.50

HERE is a screwball satire with a new slant, the story of an un-heroic hero tangling with vagaries of the home front. Soldiers have written about soldiers and civilians about civilians, but this is how *feather merchants* (civilians) look to a sergeant on fur-lough.

A frantic trip across the Middle West introduces Sergeant Dan Miller to the rigors of wartime travel. Some of it he spends under two women officers who have abused their rank somewhat and are sitting on his lap. He is witness to a USO hostess crumbling into hysteria under the impact of his appearance and he shares drinks with a maiden schoolteacher inspired to the point of song about her ribald past. Arriving home in Minneapolis, he finds his family struggling under a black-market war economy and learn-ing of war from the roller-coaster inflections of a noted news analyst. As a desk soldier, he is spurned by his hero-worshiping fiancée, Estherlee McCracken; but he gets an unexpected build-up and wakes one morning to find himself a war-bond hero. In playing the part, Dan gets into one tight scrape after another, the kind that isn't covered by G.I. regulations.

In this comic classic, outrageous episodes follow in rapid suc-cession. The Shulman fancy, so uproarious in *Barefoot Boy with Cheek,* is even more untrammeled here. Zany illustrations by William Crawford add a delightful note of idiocy to the whole proceedings.

This book has not been serialized in any form prior to this publicatio

THE FEATHER MERCHANTS

BOOKS BY MAX SHULMAN:

BAREFOOT BOY WITH CHEEK, THE FEATHER MERCHANTS

MAX SHULMAN

The Feather Merchants

ILLUSTRATED BY WILLIAM CRAWFORD

DOUBLEDAY, DORAN AND CO., INC. GARDEN CITY, N. Y. 1945

To
CAROL
my wife

Note

EVERY SOLDIER knows that "feather merchants" means civilians, but few know why it does. The origins of the term are indeed cloaked in mystery. Theories abound. Only one, however, seems worthy of even provisional credence—that of Professor Herk Bettzimmer, the famous "one-horse philologist" of Wilkes-Barre, Pa., whose testimony, you will recall, was no small factor in deciding the McCullough vs. Maryland litigation.

Says Professor Bettzimmer, "*Circa* 4500 B.C. two neighboring tribes, the Puntangi and the Snafu, went to war over the possession of a gap-toothed idol named Ed to whom they attributed widespread curative powers. At that time Ed was well concealed by the Snafu. Gluk-Os, chief of the Snafu, was taken prisoner and brought before Miklos the Scaly, prince of the Puntangi. Upon refusing to divulge the location of Ed, Gluk-Os was bound and subjected to a favorite torture of the day—tickling the soles of the feet with feathers. For weeks two shifts of Miklos's warriors tickled Gluk-Os's feet day and night, but he spoke not a word. All the feathers in Miklos's court were worn to the nub. Miklos ordered more feathers brought to him at any cost so that the torture could continue. Civilians by the thousands plucked their fowl and wives' hats and sold the feathers to the army. Hence, 'feather merchants.'

"Gluk-Os, incidentally, never did tell where Ed was hidden. The tickling bothered him not in the least, for, had the Snafu known, he was wearing history's first pair of shoes."

—M. S.

THE FEATHER MERCHANTS

CHAPTER I

I HAD a foolish feeling that everything was going to be all right as I walked up to the gatehouse at the air base. I set down my suitcase and gave the guard my furlough papers with a steady hand.

I won't deny that I had been scared stiff when I had boarded the train in Minneapolis; I had chosen a corner seat, put on a pair of dark glasses, and turned my collar up around my face. Whenever an M.P. had come through the train I had ducked quickly behind a book I had bought for concealment purposes.

The M.P.s had become less frequent south of Kansas City. South of Wichita there had been none at all. With that menace gone, I had relaxed considerably. I had opened my book and begun to leaf through it with mounting interest. It was the best-selling diary of the lady war correspondent, Hepzibah Galtz, entitled *I Been Everywhere*.

More correct than grammatical was Miss Galtz's title. This intrepid little lady had been where burros fear to tread. She was true to the credo she stated on her opening page:

"Before I left on this world assignment, my mother asked me not to go. 'Hepzibah,' she said, 'don't go.' (She is the only one who calls me Hepzibah; to everyone else I am 'Hellcat' or 'What have I got to lose' Galtz.)

"'Leah,' I answered (As you can see, I call my mother by her first name. This is only one of my unconventionalities. I am one hell of a kid.), 'my first duty is to the people. I cannot think of danger to my person, and as for my reputation, I am not one to worry about such bourgeois affectations. There's news in this here world, Leah, and I am going to get it or my name ain't "Hellcat" or "What have I got to lose" Galtz.'"

With fabulous derring-do, "Hellcat" or "What have I got to lose" explored the recesses of the world that the people might know. She scaled a perpendicular crag to interview the Grand Lama of Tibet:

"I didn't mess with him. 'Lama,' I said right off the bat, 'are you or ain't you coming in with Chiang?'

"'Daughter,' he answered, peering into my bodice, 'I'm an old man. Leave us go to my bower where we can rest.'

"With a saucy toss of my head I accompanied him to his bower. It was a rough night, and I didn't have a chance to ask him again. In the morning he was stone dead. The new Grand Lama, according to Tibetan custom, was a baby born at the exact moment of the old lama's death.

"Go ask questions from a baby."

Any hour of the day or night Miss Galtz was welcome at the homes of the great:

"'I came as soon as they told me you were here,' said Stalin. 'I was at a midnight conference with my generals, but I ran right over. Naturally I would rather be with you, "Hellcat" or "What have I got to lose," than with a bunch of stuffy generals.'

"He pinched my bottom and frisked about the room.

"'Can that crap, Joe,' I said. 'I wanna know what you're going to do about Poland after the war.'

"But before he would talk business, he made me sit down and have supper with him. We drank twenty-seven toasts to the

United Nations, and he got pretty stinking, but I know how to hold the stuff.

" 'Well, what about Poland, Joe?' I said.

"He wagged his finger at me. 'You little minx. Nobody has been able to get a statement out of me, but I'm going to tell you. Tell the American people that what I am going to do about Poland depends on a lot of things.'

"It was a clean-cut scoop for me. Boy, were Gunther and Duranty burned up!"

I had read my book and the miles had clacked by without incident. Toward the end of the trip I had actually taken off my dark glasses and exchanged pleasantries with a fellow passenger, a nasal okra grower named Minafee. When the train pulled into the station, I had gotten off with confidence. With confidence I had proceeded to the air base.

Now I stood blithely whistling the largo from *Death and Transfiguration* as the guard examined my furlough papers.

"Well, well," he said. "Sergeant Daniel Miller. We were wondering if you'd come back." He unholstered his revolver. "Let's get into the jeep, Sergeant. The provost marshal wants to see you."

The heart within me died. I climbed silently into the jeep and hung my head between my legs, maintaining that position until we reached the provost marshal's office.

"He came quietly, Captain," the guard said to the provost marshal.

"Good," answered the provost marshal. "At least we don't have to try him for resisting arrest." He dismissed the guard and motioned me to sit down. "You know, Sergeant," he said, "I've got a sister in Minneapolis."

"I didn't know, sir," I said.

"I'm sure you didn't. She sends me the Minneapolis papers regularly." He opened his desk drawer and took out several copies. "Do you recognize these, Sergeant?"

"Yes sir," I said without looking at them.

"Uh-huh. I suppose you've got a perfectly logical explanation."

"As a matter of fact, Captain, I have."

"Well, that's fine. I knew you would. Perhaps you'd like to tell it to me."

"I'd love to. But it's a rather long story."

"They always are, Sergeant. Go ahead."

"Well, sir, when I left for Minneapolis ten days ago I was just a happy soldier going home on furlough . . ."

CHAPTER II

The one-car train clacked northward through Oklahoma. From behind the green baize curtain separating the Jim Crow section of the car came the voices of darkies, as they are affectionately called in the South, droning in the throaty drawl peculiar to vitamin-D deficients. A disorganized fly beat his head wistfully against the window. I made myself comfortable on the flange of my pelvis and read an article about how you can cure syphilis in eight hours by getting into a steam cabinet and reading the *Reader's Digest*.

The sturdy little wood-burning engine chugged through the red country and part of the gray. In the shade of CCC-planted trees loose-hung farmers squatted in a position no city-bred man can even approximate and drew pictures of biological manifestations in the dirt with blunt sticks. Calico-clad farm wives, their supper sidemeat cooking in immemorial pots, sat sluggishly fanning themselves with parity checks. A turtle crossed the road to get on the other side.

With a fierce, quiet pride that American ingenuity had at last bested another loathsome disease, I finished the article and dropped the magazine to the floor. Idly I surveyed my fellow passengers. Here a child cried fitfully because he couldn't drive the train, while his mother credulously read a Superman comic book. An aging hostler smiled benignly and smote his thigh in gentle accord as his pimple-faced nephew sang "Roundup in the Sky," accompanying himself on a guitar on which was inscribed "The Ponca Kid." In front of me sat two Indians in dull, state-provided serge suits, the one next to the window trying in passionate gutturals to persuade the other to let him out in the aisle to go to the toilet.

"Dinner!" called the conductor. "First call for dinner."

Since there was no dining car on the train, an ingenious system of serving meals had been devised. As the train neared a point five miles from Dry Prong, its next stop, the conductor went among the passengers, taking their orders for dinner. Then he leaped lightly from the train, trotted ahead to Dry Prong, and had the orders ready as the train pulled in.

I placed my order, adjusted my seat to its full 85-degree incline, and settled back to await Dry Prong and dinner.

My wholesome meal of hoecake and chitterlings resting as comfortably as a bar bell in my stomach, I lit a cigarette and proceeded to read a pamphlet entitled *Babe Ruth Was Saved. Are You?* which had come tucked between two pieces of hoecake in my dinner. I reached the part where the Yankees were one run behind in the last of the ninth, two men out and one on, the Bambino was at the plate with a three-two count on him, the opposing pitcher was preparing to throw the fateful ball (the pitcher's name was not given, but I'm rather inclined to think it was George Earnshaw because of the almost tedious length of his windup), when the Babe had a divine visitation. As I raptly turned the page to discover the nature of the Sultan of Swat's disturbance at this most crucial of moments, I was suddenly interrupted.

"Is this here a good train, sojer?" asked the occupant of the seat next to mine, a lean, angular man with red dirt under his fingernails and skin like sunburned corduroy.

"No," I said.

He nodded. "Hit don't seem like a good train. Hit jerks."

He pulled out a cut plug and politely offered me the unbitten end. After I declined, he chewed off a healthy wad.

"I ain't one to wander," he continued moistly. "Born on my pap's farm—first breech-delivery baby in Oklahoma—and before now ain't never left it. 'Cept every year I go to the county fair with My Own Lucy—that's my heifer—fer the milkin' contest." He opened his coat and showed me eight blue ribbons and one red one pinned across his vest. "Won every year sincet '34. 'Cept '39. Took second that year. Governor of Iowa jedged the contest. Cain't trust a Yankee. Where you from?"

"Minnesota."

"Some's all right," he allowed. "Man and boy I stayed on thet farm sincet I was born. Hate to gad around. Travelin's all right for them as don't have lan'. Man with lan' should stay put. Married a gal from the next farm. Purty ugly. Strong though. Got a boy. Name's Billy Dickie. He's simple.

"Raise some corn, leetle okra, few beef critters. Got a mule, cistern, radio. Read the Book. Don't bother nobody. Don't nobody bother me.

"'Til last winter. Man-oovers. Sojers all over the place. Gun crew on my farm. My Own Lucy layin' there sleepin', and they use her fer a gun emplacement. Open fire. Bang. Boom. Uh-uh-uh-uh-uh-pow. Then they leave. Lucy acts funny. Won't give milk. Ain't no holes in her, but somethin's wrong. Call a vet. He looks at her. 'She's got the trauma,' he says.

"Critter ain't no good without she gives milk. I write to Washington. Git a letter back full of litacher on how to become a aviation cadet. Write another letter. This time I git a letter thankin' me fer offerin' My Own Lucy as a mascot—whatever thet is—to the Second Army but refusin' because they already got a mascot—whatever thet is—a horned toad named Topkick.

Picture of the horned toad is enclosed. My boy, Billy Dickie, he sees the picture and he gets so scared he won't sleep with the lights off fer six weeks. Burned up half a bar'l of kerosene.

"I write another letter. This time they answer thet I been accepted for aviation-cadet training.

"Thet settles it. I git on the train and go to Fort Sill. Wander around fer days talkin' to sojers. Cain't make none of 'em understand. End up umpirin' enlisted men's softball tournament. Still cain't understand thet.

"Goin' back home now. Never goin' leave again. Might's well slaughter Lucy. Damn fine heifer. Won eight blue ribbons with her. Should've won nine."

The train pulled into the farmer's station. He rose and walked sadly away. "Keep 'em flyin'," he called.

I returned to my pamphlet, found my place, and was delighted to learn that the Babe, divinely guided, poled one into the left-field bleachers, 440 feet away.

One section of the station at Wichita has been made into a USO lounge largely through the unstinting patriotism of the William Allen White chapter, Dames of Bloody Kansas, of Wichita. I made for this cheery, flag-festooned lounge as soon as I discovered that I had a two-hour wait for my Kansas City train.

I entered the lounge and nodded pleasantly to a young matron sitting at the hostess's desk reading the current *Vogue*. She began to act strangely almost immediately. The magazine dropped from her quivering hands. Her eyes darted wildly about the room. The color drained from her face.

After a moment it occurred to me why she was behaving that way. It was past midnight, we were all alone in the lounge, I was disheveled from my train ride and had a twelve hours' beard, and by her clothes and bearing it was easy to tell that she had not been brought up to spend the small hours in railroad stations with strange, disreputable-looking men.

She clenched her palms on the edge of the desk, gathering

strength. At last her USO spirit conquered her inbred revulsion, and she rose and walked toward me. Her lips moved soundlessly a few times. "Here is a ticket," she blurted finally, thrusting a small white pasteboard into my hands. Then she ran wildly to a near-by post and hung on, trembling violently for several minutes.

Having quieted down somewhat, she took several deep breaths and started toward me again. Her I. Miller-shod feet faltered as she came closer, and by the time she was at my side she was completely disorganized. "If you'll present this ticket at the soda fountain"—her voice began to rise dangerously—"YOU CAN GET COFFEE!" she shrieked and bolted away.

She tripped on the rug and lay shuddering on the floor. At length she rose slowly to her feet. She set her patrician jaw, squared her shoulders, started forward, broke down again, saved herself from falling by grabbing the back of a fortunately placed settee, pulled a cigarette from her handbag, burned up a folder of matches trying to light it, cast away the cigarette, straightened up, looked directly and unswervingly in front of her, and walked past me.

"Or a bottle of Coca-Cola," she gasped as she went by, and then she broke into a clattering sprint, skidded out the door, and ran madly down the street screaming, "Taxi! For God's sake, taxi!"

A little unnerved myself, I had a cup of coffee at the fountain and then went back to the lounge. I sank into an easy chair, picked up a movie magazine, and by the time my train arrived I learned that Myrna Loy bathes daily in pure wombat's milk, that Walter Pidgeon would sooner go out without his trousers than without his watch charm—the skull of a pygmy who saved his life some years before when Pidgeon was playing the Belgian Congo borsht circuit—and that Hollywood's current crop of divorces were all accomplished without rancor and, in fact, in all cases resulted in improved relations between the estranged parties who, in their own words, forthwith became the "best of friends."

CHAPTER III

BEFORE I came into the Army I had never been able to sleep on a train. Pullmans, I always told myself, thinking of the extra fare in terms of small-figure foulard ties and white button-down-collar shirts, were a needless luxury, if not downright un-American. So I always traveled in coaches and never slept a wink.

Losing the sleep was the least of the trouble. It was the people you ran into. I remember riding the Pennsylvania a few years back. I was in a coach occupied mainly by clean-nailed local officers of the United Mine Workers on their way to a convention in Scranton. At night, as soon as the coach lights were turned off, they fell into a slumber as untroubled as though the combined Catholic and Protestant churches, supported by unanimous and enthusiastic public opinion, had begun proceedings to have John L. Lewis sainted.

I closed my eyes and started counting sheep, but to no avail, because somehow each sheep had the face of Naomi, a machine-less-permanent-wave operator who had thrown me over two seasons before in favor of a dance-band drummer in whose single-stroke rolls she detected something fine and vital. The whole affair, as it turned out, was without satisfaction. The drummer already had a wife, an overweening wench named Babe, who ultimately persuaded him to give up the band business and take a night-school course in pharmacy.

Pitching and tossing thus, I saw a cigarette glowing in a far corner of the car. I picked my way over the recumbent labor chieftains and made for the red ash. It was a girl, I could see as I came closer. The seat next to hers was empty. I sat down and said, "I see you're having a little trouble sleeping too. Heh, heh."

She drew deeply on her cigarette, and in the resultant glow I saw the pinched, intense features of her face. She flung away her cigarette in a swift, passionate gesture.

"Mine has been a strange life," she said.

I unbuttoned my collar.

"I was an unwanted child. My father was seventy-five years old when I was born; my mother, who had married young and against the wishes of her parents, who had in mind for her a local abstract clerk named Fender, was sixty-three. Seven brothers had preceded me. The youngest was thirty-two when I was born. The next to the oldest, who suffered from a bad heart, had dropped dead upon hearing the results of the 1936 presidential election. An avid believer in the *Literary Digest,* he had wagered his wife's legacy, plus whatever he could borrow on his car, a Plymouth, on Landon to win.

"Well, there I was. My mother had become unused to children in the previous thirty years, and, moreover, her temper had grown short because of an irritating fixation of my father's that the man across the street, an inoffensive varnish remover named McIlhenny, was Judge Crater.

"To say that I was unwelcome would be understating the case. In many ways, both subtle and direct, it was made plain to me that I was an interloper. My first three years, the most formative period in my life, were a veritable hell. I was made to dress in severe black costumes. My appearance on the street was the signal for gales of derisive laughter from my fellows. All the children in the neighborhood called me 'the bastid.'

"As soon as they considered it feasible, my parents began to send me away alone on long trips. Stationmasters in far places came to recognize me, a thin, sad-eyed child carrying a well-worn valise. I stayed for varying periods with aunts, uncles, distant cousins, and occasionally, through a wrong train connection, with total strangers. Most of my hosts were frankly hostile, but even worse were some Los Angeles relatives who oozed pity and tried to convert me to membership in their religious sect, the tenets of which were diaphragm breathing and washing the feet of wayfarers, forcibly if necessary. Wherever I went I was commonly called 'the bastid.'

"This went on for years, I bounding like a cosmic shuttlecock from one coast to another, passing through the dangerous pubic years with no mother to guide me, my schooling confined entirely to the reading of Gideon Bibles, magazines abandoned in railroad cars, haphazard encyclopedias sold by aging men working their ways through colleges to relatives at whose homes I was a scarcely welcome guest. Yes, I grew bitter. Anything of flesh and blood would have.

"And then once I returned home to find myself an orphan. My father had died of a uremic disorder, gasping with his last breath, 'You fools! Crater's across the street!' My mother married Mr. McIlhenny shortly thereafter and, weakened by the excesses of a honeymoon in the winter of her life, languished and died within three months.

"At last I was free. Ha! Free! Free to do what? The habits of a lifetime, my friend, are not lightly cast aside. So here I am again, traveling to visit relatives who don't want to see me, whom I don't want to see. Free! Ha!

"But why am I telling *you* all this?"

Why, indeed?

But now, since I had joined the Army, I could sleep anyplace, trains included.

Which I did unbrokenly between Wichita and Kansas City.

CHAPTER IV

SEVERAL HUNDRED PEOPLE poured off the train at Kansas City. A single redcap stood on the platform. "Attention!" he called. "Cripples and women past sixty step one pace forward."

Whoever fell into those categories complied. The redcap collected their bags. The rest of us carried our own.

The Rocket for Minneapolis did not leave until noon, and it was only nine o'clock. I checked my bags and got shaved by a lady barber named Delilah who complimented me on the texture and consistency of my skin and mentioned that she had little, if anything, to do these evenings. Taking my pointed silence for shyness, she invited me to come up to her place for a home-cooked meal, after which she would show me how to hone a

13

razor properly. "Full many a razor has been ruined by improper honing," she said thickly, dusting my face lingeringly with talc and slipping into the pocket of my blouse a card on which was written her name, address, telephone number, and this admonition: "If not at home the first time, TRY, TRY AGAIN."

At noon the train caller announced, not without pride, that the Rocket was on time. There followed a charge of an intensity not seen since the Cimarron was opened. The train seats were filled in an instant. Nimble young men leaped into the baggage racks and were shortly joined by a contingent of lithe, long-flanked girls returning to college after the Easter holidays. Next the aisles were jammed with passengers sitting on upended suitcases. A young devotee of group singing whipped a harmonica from his pocket and started to play "Praise the Lord and Pass the Ammunition." With many cries of "What the hell. War is war," the passengers joined the singing, except for a group of marines, piled like cordwood in the rear of the car, who stoutly sang "From the Halls of Montezuma." The conductor, grown grizzled in the service of the line, came upon the scene and frankly wept.

Aloof in his Diesel sanctum, the engineer released the throttle or whatever the hell they do, and the train rolled forward.

I had just come from six months in Oklahoma, which is a dry state. In Oklahoma, if you want some whisky, you go to the nearest hotel and ask the bellboy for a pint. There is a little good-natured formality that you go through before you get it. He asks what kind you want. You say Old Schenley or Ancient Age or Four Roses or some such name. Then he goes down to the basement and finds an empty bottle of the brand you named. He fills that from his gallon jug of moonshine. He brings it to you; you give him five dollars, and after a few secretive winks and expressive smackings of lips you slink off to a dark room and bolt the swill as quickly as you can.

Frequently, as I had lain on an Oklahoma floor waiting for welcome paralysis and oblivion, I had mused about the wet and dissolute North where a man can order a highball and sit in a clean, well-lighted place sipping, smoking, making small talk, and looking out the windows at passers-by as frankly as if he lived a good life. I had promised myself that the very first time I left Oklahoma I would hit for the nearest bar to luxuriate in a resumption of what I liked to think of as civilized lushing.

Always one to keep promises of this nature, I squirmed out from under two women officers who had abused their ranks somewhat and were sitting on my lap and hacked my way to the club car.

A group of friendly revelers made room for me at their table. "Sit down, Sarge," invited a jovial, round man.

By the time we had reached the Iowa line we were all fast friends. The globular fellow who had invited me to sit down was Leo Nine, a Southern congressman and author of such legislation as the Nine-Estes bill to tax Negroes for *not* voting, the Nine-Coy bill to sell Ellis Island, and the Nine-Carruthers bill to spay schoolteachers. He was on his way to Minnesota for a farm-bloc conference where it was planned to find a new and imaginative interpretation of parity.

Miss Spinnaker, the lady in the party, was a maiden teacher of English at the Harold Stassen High School in Minneapolis. Two men completed the group—Mr. Torkelbergquist, a Minneapolis rubber-goods dealer, and Señor Rarrara, a South American commercial attaché.

The afternoon passed with drinking and conversation. Leo Nine told of crowded Washington conditions and how he himself had scarcely been able to find lodgings. Only after many days of searching, he said, was he able to sublease an apartment from three horribly scarred women who were in Washington posing for propaganda posters.

Torkelbergquist explained the rising birth rate as a consequence of the rubber shortage, speaking, out of deference to Miss Spinnaker, in oblique terms. He had grave Malthusian fears about the outcome of the situation and after a few drinks hinted delicately at regulated female infanticide.

Señor Rarrara told of his country's war effort. Their air force, he said, had lately acquired several pusher-type biplanes and the slingshots of two divisions of infantry had already been replaced with muzzle-loaders. As for their navy—Rarrara chuckled ominously—let any U-boat venture up the Orinoco and it was a dead pigeon.

I looked at posters on three sides of me which proclaimed in turn "LOOSE LIPS SINK SHIPS," "THE ENEMY IS LISTENING," and "NORTH AND SOUTH, KEEP SHUT THE MOUTH," and I said nothing.

Also silent was Miss Spinnaker. At first she listened attentively to whoever spoke, smiling or chuckling, whichever was warranted, at the proper points in the narratives. But after a bit her attention started to wander. She smiled at the wrong times and once laughed explosively as Leo Nine described the dignity of Lee's bearing at Appomattox. A little later she gave up listening altogether and began sticking her ancient legs out in the aisle to trip the colored waiters. When the waiters learned to step carefully over her sere limbs, she turned to sticking her thumb in our drinks when we weren't looking, and finally to snatching them up and drinking them.

Chivalrously, these matters were not brought to her attention. The conversation continued. Leo Nine was telling about the pioneer days when his family had crossed the frontier in an Angostura wagon. He had been born on that journey, the tenth child in the family. His father had been a scholar, he explained, and had named him Leo, which means ten in Latin. At this point Miss Spinnaker began shouting a raucous ballad entitled "Thirty Years a Chambermaid and Never a Kiss I Got." Only then was any note taken of her conduct.

"Really, Miss Spinnaker!" said Leo Nine.

"I suppose," she said, "you think I'm just a dried-up old virgin."

"Really, Miss Spinnaker!" said Torkelbergquist.

"I suppose," she continued, "you think I use a bed just to sleep in."

"Really, Miss Spinnaker!" said Rarrara.

"I suppose you think I don't know what a roll in the hay is."

"Really, Miss Spinnaker!" I said, not caring how many enemy agents heard me.

She drained all four of our glasses as we sat back aghast. "I've worked every cat house from Honolulu to Rio," she announced. "You look surprised. Well, maybe you won't be when you see a picture of how I looked in those days."

She opened her knitting bag and passed around an old daguerreotype. I am only twenty-four years old, but I know a picture of Lillian Russell when I see one.

"They called me 'Hot Helen' then. Sometimes just 'Hot.' I serviced 'em all—kings and stevedores, bankers and draymen. Jim Fisk gave me this." She showed us a trylon-and-perisphere souvenir ring from the New York World's Fair. "'Hot Jim' I used to call him."

She lit a cigarette recklessly.

"During the Bull Moose convention I did twelve thousand dollars' business in one night," she said. "That was my best night, but I had plenty almost as good. Don't worry, I've got a nice little nest egg stashed away in the Morgan bank. Old J.P.'s taking care of it for me. 'Hot J.P.' I used to call him."

A new waiter walked by, and she tripped him neatly. She reached over and sniped a drink from the next table.

"I've shilled every crooked wheel from Singapore to Hatteras," she roared. "'Lucky Lou' they used to call me. I dealt six-pack bezique to prime ministers and played the shell game with bumpkins. Arnold Rothstein gave me this." She showed us the ring again.

"'Hot Arnold' I used to call him.

"Poker, craps, dominoes, faro, blackjack, euchre, red dog—I know 'em all. Name your game, gents. I'll play any man from any land any game he can name for any amount he can count."

She rose unsteadily to her feet. "Wait'll I go to the toilet, and I'll tell you all about the days I ran Chinks over the border."

She lurched down the aisle. "I once smuggled in Sun Yat-sen. 'Hot Sun' I used to call him," she yelled over her shoulder.

She stumbled into the nearest lavatory, exiting hurriedly, speeded by the shouts of angry men.

"Well, gentlemen," said Leo Nine, "we're almost in. I guess I'll be going. Now, you all be sure to look me up when you're in Washington."

"You bet," we said.

Torkelbergquist and Rarrara left immediately afterward, each inviting me to look him up.

"You bet," I said.

After a while Miss Spinnaker came walking feebly back. She was very pale. She sank weakly into a chair. "I was told," she said, "that if you drink a tablespoon of olive oil before you begin, it doesn't affect you."

"It doesn't work," I said.

"No, I suppose not." She looked at me for a long while. "Weren't you in my English class a few years ago?"

"About ten years ago."

"Miller," she said, remembering. "Harold Miller."

"Daniel."

"Yes, Daniel. It's nice seeing you again, Daniel."

"Nice to see you too, Miss Spinnaker."

"Well, Daniel, do you still remember anything you learned in my English class?"

"I was just thinking of something I learned there, Miss Spinnaker. *The Canterbury Tales.*"

"Why those, Daniel?"

"Well, that's what we've been doing on the train—travelers telling stories to pass the time away."

"Why, so we have," she said.

She felt much better.

We were coming into St. Paul.

CHAPTER V

St. paul, and thirty minutes later Minneapolis. I pressed my nose against the window of the car as though I were a waif and there were pies outside. The thin, tame Mississippi, the green campus of the university, the lines of angry cars honking at grade crossings, the phallic grain elevators, the trackside tenements, the hissing slide into the Minneapolis station: home.

I could see Mama and Papa on the far end of the station plat-form as I got off the train. Mama was stopping every man in uniform, peering into his face, and then rejecting him with un-disguised disappointment. Papa was looking under the wheels of the train, perhaps thinking that I had ridden the rods home. Mama was beginning to accuse Papa of having come to the wrong station when they finally heard me calling them.

"My baby!" cried Mama, breaking every record for the fat ladies' 440 as she rushed toward me. "My soldier!" She threw her arms around me and started to kiss me as Papa circled around looking for my right hand to shake. "Look how skinny!" Mama wailed. "A regular skeleton. Don't they feed you? Feel, Adam, the ribs."

Papa felt. "He's in shape, that's all. A soldier."

"A shadow. A little nothing," Mama complained.

"He's strong. He looks good," said Papa stoutly.

"Half. That's all there's left of him. Half."

"He looks good," Papa maintained.

"Maybe you want to spend the whole night here on the platform?" said Mama to Papa. "Let's go."

In the car, which Papa drove with his customary casual arrogance, the subject of my lost weight was finally dropped. Mama snuggled happily against my shoulder, alternately cooing, "My baby," and asking such questions as "Who does your laundry?", "When will you be an officer?", "Can't you stay longer than a week?", and "Where is your gun?"

Papa, who groundlessly felt a rapport with internal-combustion engines, spoke only of the car. "How's she ride?" he asked rhetorically. "Smooth, eh? Just had a ring job."

He didn't know a ring from second base.

"Is gas rationing affecting you much?" I asked.

He smiled slyly and pointed at the fuel gauge which stood at the "full" mark. "I manage. I manage," he said with a smirk.

"You mean black market?" I asked in astonishment. Up to the time I left home the high point in Papa's lawlessness had been keeping a pencil that a tax assessor had forgotten at our house in 1931, and he would have returned that had not the assessor refused a request to reduce the evaluation of our Steinway on the grounds that nobody in the house could play it.

"That's against the law, isn't it?" I asked.

"Say," he said, "if they put everybody who patronized black markets in jail, there wouldn't be anybody left on the outside to keep those on the inside in."

He chuckled, pleased with his joke. Mama smiled wanly, indicating that although she had heard my father's witticism many times, she still could not deny that it was a good one.

When we were home Papa took belated cognizance of my

majority and mixed me the first highball I had ever had in his presence. Mama went into the kitchen and in a little while called me to a spread which testified that gasoline was not the only commodity these good citizens were buying on the black market. I compounded the felony.

After dinner Papa, affecting casualness, said, "Come into the den, Dan. I want to show you something."

I followed him curiously into a little room under the staircase which heretofore had not been distinguished by such a *Better Homes and Gardens*-y title as "den." This cranny had been designed into our home by an uncommunicative architect who had a miserly obsession about waste space. It was not until we had lived in the house several years that the room was discovered, quite by accident, when Papa ripped off a couple of steps after my mother's persistent complaints that she heard squirrels under the stairs at night. As it turned out, there were no squirrels under the stairs. The sounds Mama had heard were small squeals from our maid, an unprincipled baggage named Hulda, who had learned of the room and was using it to further a sordid affair with the grocer's mentally deficient but physically matured delivery boy.

Upon entering the belowstairs alcove, I saw immediately that it now deserved to be called a den. All four walls were covered with Mercator projections of the world. A huge globe stood in the center of the floor, and beside it were two leather easy chairs. In the corner was the biggest radio in Minneapolis.

"Sit down and have a cigar," said Papa, thinly disguising his pride. "It's almost time."

"Time for what?"

He held up his right hand for silence and looked at the new wrist watch on his left, like a lieutenant waiting zero hour for a bayonet charge. As the sweep second hand on his watch, which he held so that I could not miss seeing it, indicated thirty seconds until nine o'clock, he attacked the battery of dials on the formidable radio. The monster lit up like a pinball machine. After some crackling and buzzing an announcer's voice faintly said that A. K. Hockfleisch, whose acquaintance with world affairs was such that he (the announcer) felt an acute sense of inadequacy in attempting to describe it, was about to broadcast.

"I've got San Francisco," said Papa in a quiet, unboastful tone which made it clear that for this radio getting San Francisco was hardly enough to work up a sweat.

I decided not to point out that A. K. Hockfleisch could also be heard at this time over a Minneapolis station.

Now the announcer went off to a dimly lit corner to brood over his unworthiness, and the roller-coaster inflections of A. K. Hockfleisch himself were heard. At first he reviewed the day's headline news. Papa sat patiently puffing his cigar and smiling reassurance to me that this kid stuff would soon be over with and old A.K. would get down to business.

Sure enough, in a few minutes old A.K. finished his résumé of the day's news. The announcer, eager to be of some small use, rushed forward and poured him a glass of water.

"Thank you, Mr. Stooks," said the noted news analyst.

The announcer, whose name was Callahan, whimpered with gratitude that he had been remembered, even erroneously.

"Now," said A. K. Hockfleisch, "let us look at Japan."

Papa rose quickly and walked over to the Pacific Ocean wall of the room.

"The most impressive feature of the island empire of Japan," said A.K. flatly, "is its vulnerability."

"Um-hmm," agreed Papa.

"In the words of the pugilist, the little yellow man's homeland has a glass jaw," said A.K., "and people with glass jaws shouldn't throw stones."

Papa removed the cigar from his mouth, chuckled briefly, and replaced the cigar.

"But," continued A.K., in the manner of a fair-minded man who cannot blink the facts, "on December the seventh, nineteen hundred and forty-one, the beasts of the East threw the first stone. And now, by God, we are going to finish it!"

Callahan ran out to join the Marines.

"It will be a long, tough job," said A.K. gravely. "It would be doing our cause a disservice to think otherwise. But, nonetheless, Japan is vulnerable."

"Umm-hmm," said Papa.

"Her far-flung archipelago is perfectly suited to the type of warfare perfected by our Yankee fighters. Her thousands of miles of level beaches provide untold landing places. The waters around these beaches are smooth as glass all year around. Moreover, for eleven months out of the year, because of neap tides, no moon shines over Japan.

"In short, calm waters, smooth beaches, and complete darkness will make the coming invasion of Japan, to borrow a plumber's term, a lead-pipe cinch.

"But," warned A.K., "we must expect severe opposition and heavy casualties. Anyone who does not expect these things is no realist and is only hindering our war effort.

"However, we cannot deny that the little sons of heaven, bred on rice and table scraps, are no matches for our meat-eating Yanks. Even if the myopic little rats could defend their coast line, which of course they cannot, they would afford only temporary opposition to the invaders. The little yellow man has no love for the steel forged by American workers in Cleveland and Pittsburgh who, for the most part, are adhering patriotically to their no-strike pledges, although some have broken faith with their country in time of war, and if that is not treason, I should like to know what is.

"And I have not yet mentioned air power."

Papa had been frowning at the omission, but now his brow unfurrowed.

"The Jap plane is aptly named the Zero. It has *nothing*. In the last six months of fighting only two United States aircraft have been lost in the Pacific, and the destruction of one of those was due to a misunderstanding between the pilot and co-pilot as to who was driving. Our birdmen have been shooting down Jap planes like clay pigeons. Even the concussion of near misses is often enough to knock down the flimsily constructed Zeros.

"And what a target the Jap cities present for our air blasters! Their buildings, as you know, are made of rice papers and bamboo shoots. What kindling for Yank incendiaries! You will permit me a moment of levity—when our bombers drop their loads on Jap cities, there'll be a hot time in the old town tonight.

"Yes, friends of radioland, the Nips have bitten off more than their buckteeth can chew. They will live to regret December the seventh, nineteen hundred and forty-one—those who live. For a familiar battle cry is in the air. A cry to quicken the pulses of free men everywhere, a cry to strike dread into the traitorous hearts of the saffron assassins—THE YANKS ARE COMING!

"Good night, my friends, good night. Buy bonds."

The organist played the national anthem. Papa snapped to the civilian equivalent of attention. He looked disapprovingly at me sitting in my chair.

"You don't have to when it's on the radio," I explained.

"It wouldn't hurt you any," he complained mildly.

When the organist had finished, Papa turned off the radio. He cleared his throat. "The way I've got it figured," he said, "Japan is vulnerable." He pointed at the coast line with his cigar. "Look at that coast line. There's a million places where it would be child's play to land troops. We could land here, or here or here or here." He pointed out a number of reefs and shore batteries.

"Maybe we'll land at all of them at once. We've got plenty of men, best fighting men in the world, strong from eating meat. Believe me, I don't mind going without meat or gasoline or anything else so that they should have it.

"That little Jap is all through. Already he wishes he didn't start something with us. We've got him beat six ways against the middle, if I may use a card player's term.

"Of course, Dan, you mustn't be too optimistic. The Jap may be weak, but he's still treacherous. It isn't going to be quick and it isn't going to be easy. But, still, it's just plain foolish to deny the facts. We've got him beat. Anybody can see that. From now on it's just a cleanup operation.

"Now, let me tell you something about Japan's air power."

At this point Mama entered. "General MacArthur," she said to Papa, "maybe you want to keep him up all night?"

"Dan," said Papa, as though it was his own idea, "you better get some sleep. You've had a hard trip."

"Now that you mention it," I said, struggling out of my chair, "I do feel a little tired."

CHAPTER VI

I WENT UP to the sterile bedroom where I had spent one third of my life. In the corner of the room was a blond maple bed stretched out like a prim but resigned maiden. A bare-topped bureau, also of blond maple, stood against one wall. On another wall hung my college diploma and a plaque proclaiming that I was the best sport in the sixth grade—my two proudest possessions. There were six windows, three on each side of the bed, through which the winds at night crossed over my recumbent form and caused my great healthiness. The wallpaper was severe but was softened by a top border of Indian heads. The Indian motif appeared again in the curtains, bedspreads, bedside rugs, and the room's only picture, a study of an Indian who got hell beat out of him somewhere riding on a horse whose depression equaled his own. In the corner opposite the bed was a large closet smelling faintly of camphor and athletic equipment.

I opened the bottom bureau drawer and took out a pair of pajamas that I had intuitively left at home when I went into the Army. They were called Fo-To-Mon-Taj-Ies by their neurotic designer. Printed in black dye on white cloth was a montage of pho-

26

tographs of ships, bridges, houses, women, landscapes, horses, street scenes, and sporting events which covered every inch of the pajamas and gave their wearer somewhat the appearance of a fast riffle through *Life* magazine. Thus attired, I climbed blackly between the sheets and prepared to sleep off thirty hours of train riding and, if I could, six months of Oklahoma.

But Mama came in with a piece of apple pie and a glass of milk. "I thought you'd be hungry," she said.

"I was getting desperate. It's been almost three hours since I ate."

She sat down on the chair beside the bed and watched critically while I ate. "More?" she asked.

"No, thank you."

"If you don't co-operate, how can I build you up?"

"I'll force myself," I promised.

"I am going to write your lieutenant he should fix you a snack between meals. You look terrible."

Mama's preoccupation with weight was one of long standing. She was Junoesque herself in a sawed-off way, and her life had always been a model of tranquil well-being. Corpulence to her was synonymous with health and prosperity. She had been born to a rotund father and a mountainous mother who now, in their seventies, continued to enjoy flawless health and still held hands in public. Her elder brother, Felix, a cheerful, bloated fellow, after an untroubled youth had married an amiable and glandular young woman, moved to the section of Minneapolis where the old people's home was located, run for the state legislature on the one-plank platform of a three-hundred-dollar monthly old-age pension, and was now serving his fifteenth consecutive term in the statehouse. The only thin member of Mother's family was Lester, of her younger twin brothers, Chester and Lester.

Lester was the basis for Mama's weight fixation, and with cause. Chester and Lester began as identical twins, were nursed identically (Grandmother equitably rotated them), slept identical hours, laughed and cried and played identically.

But after six months a difference became apparent. Chester's baby fat solidified and multiplied. Lester, although he ate like a young bear, grew bone-thin. At the age of thirteen months Chester waddled fatly on his sausage-shaped legs. At three years he was singing tremulous ballads in kiddie revues at the neighborhood theater. Lester, on the other hand, did not even attempt to walk until the end of his third year and was stolen by gypsies at the age of five.

In primary school Chester won any number of scholastic awards and lisped his class's valedictory, while Lester became involved in a series of minor scandals having to do with the girls' locker room in the gymnasium. In junior high school Chester won a trip to Yellowstone Park with his entry in a national essay contest, a thoughtful composition entitled "If Garcia Hadn't Heard." Lester cut off his right thumb and index finger in a manual-training class. In high school Chester's ample bottom eventually filled the chair of president of the senior class. Lester persisted in a feckless romance with a janitor's defective-sinused natural daughter.

After high school fat Chester and skinny Lester went to work. Chester prospered from the first. He started as a tobacconist's clerk, saved his money, opened his own shop, then another and another and another, until at the age of twenty-three he had four, all profitable, and he married a rife and jovial blonde and settled down to a happy, fecund life. Today he is one of Minneapolis' foremost citizens and treasures an autographed picture of himself and Jack Dempsey taken when the Manassa Mauler refereed a tedious but well-attended boxing match at the Minneapolis auditorium in 1937.

But Lester! He struggled along for years selling household gadgets which he was unable to demonstrate convincingly because of his missing fingers. In the halcyon Coolidge era he was able finally to make a little money, almost in spite of himself, and he was wed to a lean and saturnine wench who dabbled in occult sciences. Two nights before the stock-market crash Lester dreamed he was roller-skating nude down an endless cobblestoned street. In the morning he told his wife of his dream. She

immediately consulted her charts and found that the dream un-
mistakably meant to buy Cities Service. Which he did with
every cent he had. The following day Lester and his wife con-
summated a suicide pact of long standing by eating poisoned
bonbons in front of a Cities Service station.

"Mama," I said, "where are you getting all this food? Don't
they use ration points in Minneapolis?"

"Points, shmoints," she said lightly. "I go to Felbgung's market and I ask Felbgung to cut me a few steaks or chops. He cuts
them for me and then I open my purse and give a look at my
ration book and I say, 'Well, well. What do you know? I haven't
got enough points.' What's Felbgung going to do, paste the steaks
back on the beef? He gives them to me."

"Mama, when you do things like that you're helping the
enemy."

"*I'm* helping the enemy? He should live so long. Didn't I give
my only son to the service? Doesn't your father buy a war bond
every week and we don't cash them in for three months? I'm a
good American. Now, you take Mrs. Farworfen across the street.
That one is a regular enemy agent. She had two miscarriages
this year, and for each one she got a ration book. And Mrs.
Rosenkavalier on Humboldt Avenue, the hoarder. She had so
much flour and sugar hidden in her house that when she had a
fire last winter, after they put it out there was a two-story cake
standing there. And Mrs. Anthrax, who lives behind the Lutheran church, the one whose husband fell out of the back window
and killed himself when he was leaning over spying into the
women's dressing room in the church the night the Ladies' Aid
put on *Craig's Wife*. I suppose you think she's not still using his
ration book. I tell you, Dan, this town is full of regular sabo-
teurs."

"What became of my ration book when I went into the
Army?" I asked.

"Maybe you would like a light snack? A toasted cheese sandwich?" said Mama, changing the subject.

"No, thanks."

"Listen, you toothpick, how can I put some meat on those scrawny bones unless you help me? I can't do it alone. From your father, that strategist, I can't get any co-operation. He pays more attention to that devil Hockfleisch than to his own wife. You should see the radio he had before this one. It cost him $1,800. I never saw so many lights and dials in my whole life. It exploded."

"Mama," I said, "I haven't been in a bed for two nights."

"All right. I'll get you a nice bowl of corn flakes and cream and then you go to bed."

"Just the bed. No corn flakes."

"Dan, what am I going to do with you?"

"I'll have two breakfasts in the morning."

"All right. Remember."

She kissed me good night and left. I curled up picturesquely in my Fo-To-Mon-Taj-Ies and fell immediately asleep.

CHAPTER VII

I was awakened the next morning by the noise of the neighbors' children shooting at each other with futuristic firearms obtained by sending tops of packages containing milled grains to radio stations. I scrounged my face into the yielding pillows, stretched my legs under the smooth linen sheets, ran my hand caressingly over the satin comforter. Ah, so soft, so smooth, so good! I had been a long time thinking about this bed. In the last weeks before my furlough I had actually begun practicing these awakening convolutions in my monastic G.I. cot. A private two bunks down saw me and started a rumor that I was smuggling in a woman at night. For a while my prestige around the camp was enormous. "Hot Dan" they called me.

After wallowing in the bed a little more I removed my Fo-To-Mon-Taj-Ies and took a shower—a private shower, all by myself. Here was something else I had dreamed of back in camp where I showered in a communal room so crowded I was never quite sure whose leg I was washing. One man in our outfit, a little guy scarcely five feet tall, tried for weeks to take a shower in that jammed room and never even got wet. For nearly an hour I

31

splashed in lone splendor in more water than falls on Oklahoma in a year.

Then I selected a natty olive-drab ensemble so popular that season, dressed, and went downstairs to a tandem breakfast of tomato juice, Wheaties with some kind of canned or fresh fruit, pig sausages, eggs, hot biscuits, and marmalade, followed by orange juice, stewed prunes, Canadian bacon, French toast, syrup, and raspberry jam. Mama watched benignly as I slid, belching, under the table.

"What do you want for dessert?" she asked.

I escaped to the living room when she wasn't looking and made my plans for the day. First there was the matter of my erstwhile true love, Estherlee McCracken. And a thorny problem that was. She had returned my last five letters unopened, the final one with a pamphlet concerning paper conservation. Estherlee was going to take some handling. I picked up the phone and dialed her number. She answered.

"Hello," I said hopefully. "This is Dan."

Silence.

"Dan Miller. I love you."

"What do you want?"

"How are you? How's your health?"

"I'm well, thank you."

"That's good."

Silence again.

"I'm fine too. That is, I was until a minute ago. I feel a chill now."

"I'm busy, Dan. What is it you want?"

"Busy with what?"

"I'm going out in a few minutes to roll bandages for the Red Cross, if you must know. For men who are *fighting* in this war."

I guess she told me all right.

"Can I see you this afternoon?" I asked.

"Impossible. I'm rolling bandages this afternoon."

"When the soldiers go out on a raid,
At home sits the young nurse's aide.
Upon their return,
Though without scratch or burn,
She'll bandage the whole damn brigade,"

I recited, vainly hoping to ease the situation.

"It's well enough for you to make jokes sitting safe in Oklahoma, but——"

"How about tonight?"

"No."

I laughed ironically, like in the movies. "This is it, then?"

"I'm afraid it is, Dan."

"Kismet."

"What?"

"Kismet."

"What's that?"

"That's Arabic for Fate."

"Where did you learn that? That's cute."

"I've picked up a lot of Arabic lately. I've got an Arab buddy at camp. Corporal Ali ben Zedrine. He gave me a burnoose. I wear it when I burn nooses. Have dinner with me tonight and I'll teach you some Arabic."

"No."

"We've meant a great deal to one another, Estherlee," I said throatily.

"It's better to break clean."

I paused the proper length of time. "Perhaps you're right."

"I am, Dan. It's better this way. You know how I feel. Nothing can change that."

"I'm sorry, Estherlee."

"It's not your fault, dear—Dan. It's just the way things worked out."

"It's certainly funny the way things worked out," I said with a short, bitter laugh.

"It certainly is."

"Then this—this is good-by."

"It's better this way."

"It's funny saying good-by like this—on a telephone, as though we've never meant anything to one another."

"It's better this way."

"I suppose you're right. Well, good-by, Estherlee. I would like to see you just once more, just to say good-by properly. But I suppose we should do it like this."

"It's better this way."

"Yes, I suppose you're right. But I can't help wishing that our good-by weren't so cold, so impersonal. Perhaps we could just have dinner tonight. What time are you through rolling bandages?"

"Five-thirty. But, Dan, I think it's better——"

"All right. I'll pick you up at the Red Cross. Good-by, dear, someone's at the door."

I hung up. Well, said I, rubbing my palms briskly, well. I'd soon put a stop to this foolishness. She was being damned unreasonable. Was it my fault if I was safe, sound, and healthy?

The night before I had left for the Army we had, as she euphemistically put it, "gone all the way." A quick, unsatisfactory spasm it had been, but, nonetheless, a major step. Weeks of conversations, reassurances, plans, vacillations, considerations, rationalizations, yeas and nays, pros and cons, had preceded the act. At length a sort of agreement had been reached, an agreement that had half negated itself during its actual consummation.

I was enlisted in the aviation cadets at that time. In June Estherlee and I were both graduated from the University of Minnesota. In other years we would have become engaged on commencement night (our romance had weathered our senior and part of our junior years), but this was Armageddon. Who could think of engagements or marriages? We had learned in the previous twenty years that nobody would survive the next war. Now we were in the next war, a just, unavoidable war, and all the young cynics turned into heroes. All values paled before this single significance: the young, strong men (among them, I) were going off to war. It was a time of tragic magnificence, as any fool could plainly see.

I waited through that summer for my induction orders. During the days I went around doing little kindnesses for people so that they would remember me favorably when I was dead. The nights were spent with Estherlee in hot, desperate clinging. Bravely we talked about how dulcet and decorous it was to die for one's country. From our morbid convictions it followed naturally that we deserved a little of the *summum bonum* before it was too late; would, in fact, be remiss not to take it. So we talked and necked and hemmed and hawed and needled one another into emotional turmoils until the night before I left, when we finally agreed that my certain destiny outweighed the moral considerations. In spite of gnawing last-minute doubts and fantastic inexperience on her part and acute nervousness on mine, it was done. I went off dry-eyed to war.

For three weeks I was an aviation cadet. As eager as any of them, I bounded from my bed at reveille, learned to salute, drill, march, and sing the Air Corps song, did calisthenics that previously I had seen only on the Orpheum circuit, ran around the camp during my off-duty hours to develop my wind, read nothing but aircraft-silhouette books, and took ice-cold showers. By God, I said, feeling my flabby muscles congeal, I'm going to get some of them bastards before they get me.

Then I was washed out on a slight technicality—something about I couldn't see.

I was transferred to the Air Force ground forces and sent to a new Oklahoma airfield from whose outraged topsoil cotton had been rooted out only a few weeks before. I was a member of a "cadre" (from the Latin *cadere*, meaning it shouldn't happen to a bachelor of arts). Living and working in a buildingless, roadless camp, our job was to get the field organized for a complement that would arrive some months later.

Our lieutenant was a nice, inarticulate guy who had been scoutmaster of a troop in Chagrin Falls, Ohio, for ten years prior to entering the Army, and during that decade his troop had taken six firsts and three seconds in state-wide fire-by-friction contests. One year the troop did not compete because of the untimely indisposition of its star incendiary and anchor man, Harold (Blazes) McNachnie. The contest that year was held on the day before Easter Sunday, and on that day McNachnie, a religious fanatic, always suffered from bleeding palms.

The lieutenant was no mean fire-by-frictioner himself. Scorning cigarette lighters and matches alike, he always kept in his desk drawer some sticks and thongs with which he lit his cigarettes. The lieutenant's cigarette-lighting impedimenta, by the way, afforded him a heap of innocent merriment. When you came into his office he would take a handful of thongs out of his drawer and say, "Do you know what these are?"

You would say, "Thongs."

To which he would answer, "You're welcome," and his pale blue eyes would dance with deviltry behind tortoise-shell glasses.

But I digress. I was saying that I was a member of a cadre and our lieutenant was a nice, inarticulate guy. He considered it a matter for rejoicing that we were the first arrivals on the field. Occasionally he would call us together and say in his sincere, halting manner, "Men, I don't know what you think about being here—that is, I'm sure you have your own ideas—but, well, to me it's something admirable. Admirable, in that it is to be admired. I mean this mud and everything and nobody is here yet, except, of course, we are here, and maybe there are no streets or buildings—I say 'maybe.' Of course there aren't. I, and all of you, too, of course, can see that—and maybe we do sleep in empty Garand cases. But what I feel is that we're all lucky to be here now when there is nothing. I realize, of course, that there are certain hardships or difficulties to be endured or undergone, that is, comparatively speaking. By comparatively I mean compared to later when we have beds and barracks and real company streets. But, on the other hand, I look at it this way: we are pioneers, in a sense. We will see this post grow and the blue skies above it— of course they are gray at this time of year, which is winter, no matter how mild it seems to a Northerner like me, and, of course, many of you, but I can promise you, barring, of course, unseasonal weather, that in summer they, the skies, I mean, will be, as I said, blue—we will see in the skies, blue or gray, depending on the season, the planes of the Army Air Forces, and we will know—those of us who are still here, for you can never tell in the Army—that this cadre's groundwork made it all possible."

Then we would give him three cheers and a tiger, hoist him to our shoulders, and carry him around the mud for a time singing the Air Corps song. At length with mock severity he would order us to let him down and go into his office and light a few fires as he always did when he was pleased.

The scoutmaster was right. The camp grew, and the barracks, row on row of livable eyesores, sprang up. Concrete was poured over the insurgent cotton, and soon there was a runway around the camp. Black-topped company streets wound their way through the mire; before long it got so a man could finish a day's work with clean shoes. The camp, before our eyes, perceptibly, took shape.

When my college-weakened eyes had eliminated me from the aviation cadets and put me into the ground forces I had felt about as useful as a rotolactor in a bull pen. I thought they were going to make a mechanic out of me, and I knew that if the outcome of the war depended on my so much as changing a spark plug, Hitler would soon be eating dairy lunches in the White House. When they wisely gave me a clerical job, I considered suicide. In my righteous, civilianish opinion, a soldier who held a desk job was a slacker, unless he was deathly ill, and such I suspected of malingering. I soon learned that you don't put ten million citizens in an army and get them where they have to be, fully trained and fully equipped, without a million miles of paper. Every spoon in every mess kit and every Flying Fortress has to be accounted for. All the trivia, all the data, have to be on paper, to be sifted and sent higher up, resifted and sent still higher, and so on until the silver-starred boys in map-covered rooms like my father's den can move colored-headed pins around and know that what each pin represents is going to be where that pin is sticking. It can't be done any other way, and each soldier who types, files, and records papers is in every sense a soldier. I learned my work and learned it well; my rapid promotions proved that.

But there was a little trouble about persuading Estherlee. Here she was, sitting in Minneapolis, trying to convince herself that our last night was something fine and beautiful and waiting for my death notice to square her conscience. And here were my letters coming from bombproof Oklahoma: "Darling, today I was promoted to private first class." "Darling, today I was promoted to corporal." "Darling, today I was promoted to sergeant." "Darling, today I'm real busy getting out a survey of non-expendable office supplies." "Darling, today I cut my finger on the edge of a piece of paper. I went to the infirmary and they put some sulfa on it, and it feels better already. Isn't sulfa wonderful?"

Estherlee sat there waiting for "The War Department regrets" and I sent her news of promotions and cut fingers. She got hotter and hotter, and her letters got colder and colder. In her last one she said, "You must be feeling proud of yourself sitting there in Oklahoma at your safe job and knowing that you got what you wanted from me."

"I should live so long, Estherlee," I wrote back, "that little episode is all forgotten. It means nothing to me."

I must have said something wrong because after that she started sending my letters back unopened.

Well, I guessed I could straighten things out at dinner. And now I had the whole afternoon free, and Mama was coming from the kitchen with a plate of sandwiches. I hurriedly decided to visit the campus.

"Eat. Eat, you skeleton. Where you running?" she cried.

I meshed the gears in Papa's newly ringed, gas-filled car and drove off.

CHAPTER VIII

How GREEN WAS MY CAMPUS that afternoon! Emerald, serene, eternal, it sprawled on a bluff overlooking the Mississippi. I had plenty of time to drive around and look at it because it took me better than an hour to find a parking space. All the campus parking lots were jammed. "More students drivin' now account of the war," a traffic cop explained to me. Parked at last, I proceeded on foot across the campus.

First I wandered across the Knoll, in the good years a verdant, tree-covered acre which had served as a lunch and trysting place. Now leggy coeds flexed and posed, apparently to keep in practice, because, except for a few underage freshmen, there were no men in sight. Emboldened by sharp, two-noted whistles and undeniable winks, I stopped and talked to a group of four coeds. "Nice day," I said.

"It certainly is, Lieutenant," cooed one, smiling and wiggling late pubic acquisitions.

"This spring weather," sighed another, slithering sinuously over the grass. "It does something to me. Does it do something to you, Captain?"

"I feel so kind of cuddly and lovely, Major," a third confessed, debarking a young spruce with her writhing back.

The fourth went all out. "Colonel," she panted, "let's."

I escaped with bruises and continued my walk around the campus. In front of the library I met a lean, thin-haired young man named Blodgett who had been in my senior composition class the year before. At that time, I remembered, he had been writing a trilogy. The three novels were called *Flesh, Lust,* and *Venery;* the entire trilogy was entitled *Spasm.* It was a study of the aphrodisiac effects of crowding people into streetcars.

The hero, Jason Johnson, is a streetcar conductor who is unable to please his wife in the evenings because of erotic aberrations during his day's work. In the first book the Jason Johnsons are worried about the apparently causeless breaking up of their marriage. To save their home they try various stopgap remedies, such as reading aloud to one another and painting decals on the kitchen cupboards. But all measures fail, and the end of the first book finds them, puzzled but estranged, in a court of equity.

In the second book they go their separate ways. She attends law school, is admitted to the bar, becomes involved in a paving scandal with an unscrupulous contractor named Mac Adam, and is banished from the town. He, through a series of preposterous errors, delivers a lecture on papal fallibility to a Knights of Columbus picnic and is nearly stoned to death. Needless to say, the Johnsons are both miserable.

In the third book Jason hears that his wife lies ill of an intestinal complaint in a neighboring town. At this time he is penniless because of a disastrous week end at the whippet races, to which, in his moral disintegration, he has become addicted.

Heedless of consequences, he absconds with his day's streetcar receipts and rushes to the side of his ailing wife. She, however, is past hope. What is worse, in her delirium she fancies that he is the appellate court judge who denied her a writ of certiorari during her paving litigation. She dies calling down curses on him.

Meanwhile a cordon of police breaks into the room to arrest him for the theft of the streetcar proceeds. Feigning a call of nature, he goes into the bathroom to commit suicide. He hopes to find something lethal in the medicine cabinet; there are only suppositories. He eats one or two of them, but their effect, if anything, is salubrious. Frustrated, defeated, broken, his life ruined by something he cannot even comprehend, he goes out and surrenders to the police. The crowning irony is that now he *really* has to go to the toilet, and he's embarrassed to ask them again.

"Well, Blodgett," I said, "how's the trilogy? Found a publisher yet?"

"I've given it up," he answered. "From now on I'm through writing significant stuff. I've gone commercial. I want to get my hands on some of that big money that's floating around. I would have, too, if things hadn't gone wrong."

"What happened?"

"I was classified 4-F."

"How did that upset your plans?"

"I was all set to write a book about the Army. Like Hargrove. I had the thing almost done. All I needed was to get in the Army. I had the characters all chosen, the situations all set. Sure-fire stuff. I had a sergeant—a big tough guy with a face like a bulldog, tough-talking, but a heart of gold. I had a private—dumb and innocent, a guy who did everything wrong, but lovable. I had a million laughs like this one: the soldiers are assembled by a river, and the sergeant says, 'Fall in,' and this dumb private falls in the river, and the sergeant says, 'What did you do that for?' and the private says, 'You said, "Fall in," didn't you?' I had a million laughs like that one, one right on top of another.

"And in spite of the horseplay and hilarity in the book, I had a Message. I was going to show how you get all these different types into an army camp—farmers from Iowa, subway guards from New York, movie actors from Hollywood, cotton pickers from Georgia, all kinds of people—and after you train them a few months all their differences disappear, and they're all the same, single-minded American fighting man.

"But they classify me 4-F, and I'm stuck. Nobody will read a book about soldiers by a civilian. So here I've got a million dollars' worth of characters and sure-fire gags—with a Message to boot—and I can't do a thing with it."

"That's rough," I said. "The world is waiting for stuff like that."

"Say," he said, looking crafty, "you used to write a little. How about selling you some of this stuff? I got a million gags. Listen: the sergeant says, 'Present arms,' and the private gives the sergeant his gun, and the sergeant says, 'What did you do that for?' and the private says, 'You said to present arms, didn't you?' There's just no end to them, Dan. Gag, gag, gag, one after another. This book will make you a rich man. Civilians are buying all the army books they can get their hands on. Soldiers amuse hell out of civilians."

I thanked him kindly and refused. "If I write a book," I said, "it will be about civilians. Civilians amuse hell out of soldiers."

"Oh well," he said philosophically, "I'll get rid of them somewhere. I can't be crying over spilt milk. I've got work to do. I'm writing a book now that should make me a million dollars. I'm going to scoop the whole world. My book will come out the day the war ends. It will be the first book debunking the war. I'll tell all about the munitions makers' profits and the shady military purchasing deals and the bad generalship and the faulty equipment and the debauchery of army officers and homosexualism in the ranks and the fake atrocity stories and the needless amputations in army hospitals and the biggest hoax of all—the war never had to be fought."

"I've got an appointment," I said.

I resumed my tour of the campus. There were coeds everywhere. Some leaned against buildings. Some hung out of windows. Some sat in convertibles with motors running (both the convertibles' and the coeds'). Some fidgeted on the grass. All kept their eyes peeled for the infrequent male—the draftproof aeronautical-engineering student, the medical student finishing his course under army sponsorship, the seventeen-year-old freshman, the bald or balding professor.

One of the last-named fell in beside me as I walked. "I won't deny," he said, guessing what I was thinking, "that at first I was pleased by all this. To be whistled at, jostled against, and mentally undressed by an attractive young woman is flattering. I am still a young man, relatively speaking, and I am still a sound man biologically if I exercise prudence. It is not unpleasant to be the object of such lascivious overtures, and there is some poetic justice in it too.

"In previous years I used to stare at these girls and think my thoughts, and when I reached the boiling point, as it were, I went to an understanding trollop who served me at these times. I never resented the indifference of the coeds, their obliviousness to my feelings. To be sure, I concealed my feelings, for I am a man of dignity. But nonetheless, when a younger man lusted after one of these young women, no matter how well he disguised his passion, she always was aware of it and acted accordingly. But I—when I saw them rolling a stocking or settling a twisted breast in its harness (braziers, I believe they are called), they would proceed with their tasks as unhurriedly as though a glimpse of thigh or mammae had no more effect on me than on a hall tree.

"But, as I say, I did not resent that. I am a teacher to whose care the young are entrusted for learning. I considered it an oblique tribute to my excellence as a teacher that these young women did not think of me as a man. Nevertheless, I was gratified at first when I became one of the few remaining men on the campus and cognizance was taken of my gender at last. Now when I see them rolling a stocking they hoist their skirts down with alacrity. But now they roll their stockings whenever they think I'm looking.

"At first, I say, I was gratified. But soon it became disconcerting. I have neither the money nor the strength to make all the visits to my friend that I have felt the need for in recent months. And to make advances to a student is unthinkable. Caught between the Scylla of excitement and the Charybdis of age plus a fixed income, I am going to pot.

"I have offered my services to the Army, but they informed me that the demand for experts in Byzantine architecture is slack at this time and that no boom is anticipated."

He stopped in front of a lecture hall.

"Now," he said, "I am going to give a lecture. There is one man in my class, a frail youth whose health precludes military service. God grant that he is well enough to be here today so that I may fasten my eyes on him and thus be able to deliver my lecture. I cannot stand much more of breast and leg and hot, mascaraed eyes. Good-by, young man. Buy bonds."

He turned into the lecture hall and I continued my circuit of the campus, sighing softly, "Ichabod. The glory has departed."

CHAPTER IX

I WAS IN FRONT of the Red Cross office at precisely five-thirty. She was just coming out the door. My heart slipped into a Cheyne-Stokes routine. I did not try to conceal my satisfaction as I watched her walk across the sidewalk to the car. In ten years a Lane Bryant customer without a doubt, but now—five feet three, 125 pounds, black hair, blue eyes, small nose, small mouth, pointed chin, milk-white skin, high, disassociated breasts, narrow waist, a pelvis that could accommodate a pair of water jugs, full-calved legs which filled her Nylons so completely that if you tried to gather a pinch of stocking between thumb and forefinger you would fail, narrow ankles, size 4-AAA shoes. She was wearing a small, dark, veiled hat cocked low over one eye, a dark blue silk dress which billowed demurely where it didn't matter, clung brazenly where it did.

"You look wonderful," I said with the whole heart.

She got into the car. If I had thawed her over the phone in the morning, she was frozen again now. "I tried to call you to break this date, but you weren't home. I think it would have been better if we hadn't seen each other tonight," she said.

"Nonsense," I protested. "We're a couple of civilized, intelligent people. We can say our good-bys properly."

"Well, just dinner then. After that you'll take me right home?"

"As you say. You're looking lovely, Estherlee."

"Thank you. You've lost weight."

"Oh, have I? My mother says I've gotten hog-fat. She's put me on a skim-milk diet."

We spoke carefully of trivial things as I drove out to the Longhorn, a suburban steak house of poignant associations. "Our place," we had always called it. Actually it was owned by two lowbred Slovenes named Hrdlicka and Czyncz who freely practiced wife trading and whose numerous offspring presented vexing problems in paternity. In fact, one boy, Basil, was the child of neither. His father was a somnambulist named Harris who wandered one night from his next-door lodgings into the bedchamber of Mrs. Czyncz. She, thinking it was Czyncz or Hrdlicka, made no commotion.

There are those who say that Harris wasn't sleeping.

The Longhorn had been the scene of our first kiss. It happened one evening when we were double-dating with my friend Sam Wye. At this time I had been going with Estherlee a couple of months, but I had held myself in check because I had been warned that she had Puritan tendencies and I didn't want to lose a girl whose dimensions so delighted my middle-European tastes by making premature advances. We were sitting in the Longhorn eating steak, the four of us. Somewhere Sam Wye had picked up a girl with a cleft palate and he was telling her harelip jokes. (A mischievous character, Sam Wye. Last I heard, he was in an engineers' battalion. I was happy to learn that he was on our side.) After a while Sam got tired of baiting his girl and turned to Estherlee. "The trouble with you," he said, "is that you're frigid."

"What?"

"Frigid. A lady eunuch. You'll probably turn into an elecdrip."

"A what?"

"An elecdrip. A drip who goes around parking places at night shining spotlights into parked cars. You might even become a policewoman."

That stung her. "Frigid, am I?" she said. "Do you call this frigid?"

Whereupon she kissed me full on my sirloin-filled mouth. From then on it was easy.

After that we came to the Longhorn often. It was at the Longhorn that we made our final decision on my last night at home. Leaving our steaks half finished, we drove to near-by Lake Echo, where on the grassy shores of a dark inlet I ruined her life.

I parked the car in front of the Longhorn and we went in. I steered her to a dark corner booth that had been our favorite. A waiter laid menus on the table. The menu was unchanged from the last time I had seen it except for doubled prices and these two notices penciled on the bottom by Hrdlicka, the partner who could write: "On Account of the Duration, You Only Get One Pat Butter" and "Don't Get So Huffy If the Service Is Slow. How Do You Know Maybe Your Waiter Gave a Quart Blood This Afternoon?" We ordered the house's special, *filet mignon Hrdlicka et Czyncz*.

During dinner I did not speak, not wishing to interrupt the flow of memories that I hoped the Longhorn was awakening in Estherlee's mind. She, too, was silent, which I held to be a good sign. After dinner we lit cigarettes and I blew smoke rings, an accomplishment that in the past had never failed to delight her. Still unspeaking, I paid the check and we went out to the car.

With confidence in the mnemonic effects of the Longhorn, I boldly swung the car toward Lake Echo. "Dan," Estherlee, that fox, said, "you are driving to Lake Echo. You promised to take me home right after dinner."

"I just thought we could talk for a few minutes."

"Please take me home."

"But it's so early. Can't we go someplace for a little while?"

"We have nothing to talk about. I want to go home this minute."

"Aw, Estherlee."

"I'm sorry I ever consented to this date, although, to be sure, I have no recollection of so doing. I don't believe you intended to say good-by at all tonight. If you think you can talk me out of anything, you're wasting your time and mine. My mind is made up. I am trying to be civil and not bring up painful matters. Now you will please take me home."

"We could go someplace and dance."

"No."

"Canoeing."

"No. Turn the car around and take me home."

I saw the lights of a movie theater a block ahead. "The point is," I said, "that you don't want to have any conversation with me this evening."

"Exactly."

"We couldn't very well talk at a movie, could we?"

"No, but——"

We were in front of the theater. I quickly pulled into a parking space. "All right," I said, applying Judo and escorting her from the car. "Come on." I had her prudently wedged in the center of a crowded row before she could protest. "Dan!" she said.

"Shh," said a man beside her.

She leaned back sullenly in her seat. The newsreel was on. First there were pictures of a jeep demonstration during which the versatile little vehicle climbed up a perpendicular cliff, forded a stream twenty feet deep, and finally, driverless, smashed into the jungle and rounded up one hundred and twenty Jap prisoners.

Then there was a representation of a recent air battle. The newsreel commentator said with perfect frankness that no *actual* pictures of the battle were obtained, but that the scenes to follow would give the audience a superb conception of what took place during the battle. There followed a sequence from *Hell's Angels*, with Spads and Fokkers chasing each other the hell all over the sky, pilots getting shot and immediately releasing a neat trickle of chocolate syrup from the corners of their mouths, the same plane being shot down in flames three times, and occasional glimpses of the late Jean Harlow where the film editor had been careless.

Finally came the cheesecake, this time a scene of Hollywood starlets (by coincidence, all under contract to the company which produced the newsreel) who were having the names of their favorite soldiers tattooed on their upper thighs. One, who was being groomed for speaking roles, explained demurely, "When Hymie comes marching home, I want him to see that I've been thinking of him."

Next the feature came on. It was a war epic entitled *Murder the Bastards*. Because of the patriotic nature of its subject, the Hays office had blinked the title. Its stars were Omar Beasley, a decaying juvenile originally brought to Hollywood by David Wark Griffith, and, in her first American role, the sensational foreign discovery, Philomene Noodnik, who for years had played the lead in the annual Sofia drama festival, a week-long cycle of tableaux depicting the discovery of buttermilk by Hunrath the Bald, a twelfth-century Bulgar princeling. When her country fell into the Axis orbit Philomene escaped to Lisbon disguised as a clothes hamper. She was fortunately able to book passage to America on the Clipper. She learned English on the flight across from a friendly co-pilot named Ralph. He did not give his last name.

As *Murder the Bastards* opens, a Flying Fortress is winging over the Pacific. Inside is the crew, Omar at the pilot's seat. The crew is making small talk over the interphones. Everyone is relaxed except Ed, the waist gunner, who keeps saying he's too young to die. The navigator takes a reading and announces, "Ten minutes from target."

"Take over," says Omar to the co-pilot, and goes back to give his crew a final check. He says a few encouraging words and pats each man on the shoulder. Each replies with a confident smile, save Ed, who falls to the floor kicking and screaming. Omar goes into the back end of the fuselage to inspect the wiring and is astonished to see a woman half hidden behind an oxygen tank. She is Philomene, a half-caste with whom Omar has been trifling back at the air base. "You!" he cries. "What are you doing here?"

"I make sky-tiffin for you," she says, writhing sinuously at his feet.

"Good heavens," says Omar, "you can't stay here. This is no place for a woman."

"I don't be much bother," she pleads. "I sweep up a leetle, keep the jernt nice and clean."

The navigator breaks into Omar's dilemma. "One minute from target."

"Two minutes ago you said ten minutes from target," Omar says testily.

"So I made a mistake," says the navigator. "Whatsa matter, you never made a mistake?"

Omar rushes to his seat just in time to pilot the plane over a Jap supply dump. The bombs are dropped and all hit squarely. In a minute the sky is filled with Jap fighter planes. They seem to be using Spads and Fokkers. There is an occasional glimpse of Jean Harlow. Inside the Fortress the crew has manned machine guns. Every thirty seconds one of them yells, "I got the bastard!" and there is a shot of the same plane going down in flames. Ed, his mouth working, makes an attempt at handling his gun but gives up in a few minutes and falls down whimpering, "I'm scared, I tell you, scared." Philomene takes over his gun and soon shouts happily, "I got, how you say, the bastard!"

But the Fortress is no match for all the enemy Spads and Fokkers. The fuselage is ripped with bullets, the wings are perforated, and one by one each motor is shot out. "Prepare for crash landing," says Omar. He doesn't know it yet, but everyone else except Ed and Philomene has been killed. He brings the plane down in a fortunately placed meadow in the middle of a jungle.

The three survivors wander for days in the jungle, Philomene making scant tiffin of grubs and wild berries. Ed's nerves, although it seems hardly possible, get even worse. One afternoon he loses control completely and begins screaming at the top of his lungs. "Quiet, you fool," says Omar. "Do you want to bring every Jap in the jungle down on us?"

Maybe Ed didn't want to, but the next minute the Japs are all around them and trundle them off to headquarters.

Inside headquarters sits the Jap colonel, played by Sidney Fatstreet, eating grapes off the tip of a dagger. "Aha," says Sidney. "Still trying to thwart the Japanese Empire, I see."

"Oh yeah," says Omar.

"When will you democratic fools learn that your system of government is decadent?"

"Oh yeah," says Omar. "Democracy is the right to boo the Dodgers. Democracy is the smell of popcorn, the golden wheat fields rippling in the western breeze, the Sunday movie, the corner drugstore, the mailman's whistle, the shucking bee and the quilting party, the letters to the editor, the torchlight parade, the new, gleaming cities, the tall forests, the kid on the bike. Democracy is the right of every man to stand up and speak his mind, just as I am doing now."

"Very nicely said," says Sidney. "But you can't win. The new order is on the march; a new world is in the making. Only the strong and the ruthless shall survive, and that is as it should be."

"Oh yeah," says Omar.

"I would like to continue this discussion," says Sidney. "I enjoy your command of language. But, unfortunately, time does not permit. Right now I would like some information. We have reason to believe that the Americans are planning an invasion of this island. You can tell us when. You tell us, and we will send you to a nice, restful detention camp. Refuse and you die."

"I'll tell," cries Ed.

Omar whips out a revolver which he had concealed in his tunic and kills Ed.

"For that you die," says Sidney. "Take him away. Leave her here."

Omar is thrown into a barbed-wire stockade. At the end of several hours Philomene is brought in looking raped. "The bastards," says Omar. "The *bas*tards!"

"I did not tell them," she says.

"Good girl," he says.

It is obvious in another minute that she couldn't have told them even if she had wanted to because she didn't know. For he proceeds to tell *her* the plans. It seems that the Americans are going to make a landing that very night. They are figuring on a surprise landing, but it appears that the Japs are ready for them. "I've got to warn them," says Omar.

A guard walks by. "What time you got, buddy?" asks Omar.

"Eight-thirty," says the guard.

"Nice wrist watch you got there," says Omar.

"Oh, it's nothing," the guard answers.

"Let's take a look at it."

"O.K.," says the guard. He sticks his hand through the barbed wire. Omar grabs his wrist, while Philomene reaches through, draws the guard's dirk, and cuts his throat.

They rush back to the beach. On the horizon the United States invasion fleet can already be seen. The Japs are dug in on the beach. The Yank invasion barges come closer to the shore. "They'll be ambushed," Omar whispers. "We've got to let them know."

They spot a Jap gun emplacement, creep across the sand, and overpower the two Jap gunners, apparently a pair of mutes. The barges are coming closer, closer. Omar opens fire, turning the gun on the Jap positions. He gets a goodly number of the bastards. The barges turn back. A Jap sneaks up from behind and throws a grenade at Omar and Philomene.

When the smoke clears they are lying in the dugout neatly bleeding to death from the corners of their respective mouths. "It's funny going like this," says Omar. "I used to think of taking you back to my little chicken ranch in Jersey. Got some fine chickens out there, Bearded White Silkies, Naked Necks, Mottled Houdans, Dark Brahmas, and Silver Sebright Bantams. Got a little white cottage with a picket fence and chintz curtains. You'd have loved it."

"I—I would have make tiffin for you," she breathes, sinking fast.

"Yes, you—you would have made tiffin for me."

They kiss bloodily.

"Good-by," he says.

"Good-by," she answers.

They die.

Meanwhile the Yank invasion forces regroup and attack the island from the other, undefended, side. There follows a tremendous battle, including some more shots from *Hell's Angels*. By morning the island is in American hands. The finale is a cloud shot with ghostly figures of Omar and Philomene smiling and waving from a two-seater Spad. In the background is a soupçon of Jean Harlow.

Estherlee and I went out of the theater and into the car. "Some movie," I said deprecatingly.

Her eyes flashed, and I noticed for the first time that they were wet. "I didn't think," she said hotly, "that you'd gotten so low that you'd make fun of *other* people dying for their country. Now take me home."

There was clearly no use arguing now. I took her home, walked her to the door, where she deftly slipped out of a clinch and left me dejected on the stoop.

"I'll think of something," I mumbled as I drove home.

CHAPTER X

MY GREAT-AUNT PLACENTA, a fretful woman who was born with a caul, used to say that one never knew where he would be tomorrow. "One never knows where he will be tomorrow," was the way she put it. To illustrate, she would tell an anecdote about the time in 1898 when she was riding a train back from Rochester, where she had gone to consult Dr. Will Mayo about a muscular condition caused by sleeping in too short a bed. At Plain Dealing, Minnesota, the train pulled off on a siding to make way for a mercy train bearing a load of ipecac to stricken Lac Qui Parle, a French community whose residents lay in beds of pain after a Bastille Day celebration during which they had consumed vast quantities of wine made by the local vintner, an untidy Parisian named Jacques le Strap, who had neglected to remove his stockings before tramping out the grapes. Aunt Placenta's car, the last on the train, somehow got uncoupled and was left on the siding when the train resumed its journey. Through some incredible mischance it was hooked onto a passing Northern Pacific bound for Nome, Alaska. Before the error could be rectified Aunt Placenta was in Nome, at that time a boom town jammed to bursting with prospectors. No fool she, she opened a saloon with six bottles of liniment that Dr. Will Mayo had given her.

She prospered immediately. Before long she was living with her faro dealer, a dextrous Eurasian named Chinese Gordon, who ultimately diddled her out of the bulk of her substance, leaving her only enough to get back to Minneapolis and buy an electric car on which she had painted "MEN STINK."

I recalled Aunt Placenta's words about the inscrutability of the future the next morning at five-thirty as I sat in a boat on Lake Winnihoopah fishing for crappies with Sam Wye. He had come into my bedroom at 4 A.M. carrying fishing rods and a tackle box and singing a sea chanty about a shad's change of life entitled "No Mo' Roe." He had informed me that he was on a three-day furlough before he went overseas with his engineers' company and that he wanted to do the things he loved best—fishing and drinking. Nothing loath, I went along.

And here we were, on a cool, gray, choppy lake under a dawning gray sky, with a gunny sack full of beer tied to the end of the boat, a package the size of a wardrobe trunk ("Lunch," Mama had explained) in the bottom of the boat, and the crappies were biting. Sam looked happy and fit. His shoulders had broadened in eighteen months of engineer's training, and his bucktoothed, mischievous, squirrel's face was brown underneath his crew haircut.

Hundreds of previous trips had taught us the fish haunts of Lake Winnihoopah. We pulled up fat crappies as quickly as we could fix minnows to our hooks and drop the lines back into the water. When we had our limit of crappies we moved to a weedy inlet and cast for bass. Sam got three and I got two. Now the sun was high. We rowed out to the deep middle of the lake, attached June-bug spinners and weights to our lines, let out about thirty feet, put the oars inside the boat, took off our shirts, opened two bottles of beer, and drifted. "Ah," said Sam.

"Ah," said I.

I was enjoying myself while I could because I knew that

somehow, before this day was over, something bad would happen to me. Except for the night he had goaded Estherlee into kissing me for the first time, no good had ever come to me from Sam Wye. Not that he wasn't my friend; he probably liked me as well as anyone. It was just that the mischief which governed his every action was completely impersonal. Anyone who was around Sam long enough—a whole day, for instance—would get involved in his machinations. Not even his own mother and father were exempt. Those two had been living acutely incomplete lives since Sam had convinced them that normal relations past forty result in curvature of the spine.

His dog, Nero, was also a study in neurosis. By walking past Nero every day for weeks with a plate of hamburger, then going into his room, closing the door, and purring, Sam had persuaded the hapless beast that he was discriminating against him in favor of a cat. He further rocked Nero's sanity by feigning inadvertence and calling him Kitty.

Sam's torts against me included signing my name to letters he sent to the Atlanta *Constitution* urging the practice of miscegnation, alienating a young woman with whom I was making good progress by telling her that all my forebears were midgets, and prevailing upon me to make a fourth in a quarter-of-a-cent bridge game with three strangers who he knew full well were a touring bridge-exhibition team. On these occasions and many more I had soberly considered breaking with him, but with a world full of dullards, you don't cast off Sam Wyes.

I wondered idly, as we drifted and drank beer, what Sam had in store for me this day. "Sam," I asked, "how are you planning to wrong me today? Or haven't you got any plans; are you just figuring that some opportunity will come up?"

He finished his bottle before he answered. "Pal, you got me wrong. You'll find me a changed man: I've given up needling people for the duration. It's part of my austerity program."

I hooted.

"Really. I've been in the Army long enough to have learned

that unprincipled frivolity is not becoming in times like these. It is a duty I owe to my brothers in arms."

"Tell me more," said I, reeling in a catfish and throwing it back with alacrity. Until I went South I didn't know that people ate catfish. The Minnesota Game and Fish Commission spends more than a million dollars a year just to teach catfish to swim out of the state. Catfish, okra, turnip greens, sorghum.

"How unseemly it would be," continued Sam, "for me to pursue the irresponsibility that characterized my undrafted years when the men about me have forsworn all but grimness. Let me give you an example."

"Say, I wish you would," I said. And they *fry* steaks. Hookworm, freight-rate discrimination, Ku Klux Klan, boll weevil, lynching, erosion—what can they expect if they eat catfish and *fry* steaks?

"One night a few weeks ago I was lying on my bunk in the barracks contemplating some mayhem. A few of the men were in a corner talking. I half listened to what they were saying, and then suddenly it struck me. I gave up my nefarious thoughts and turned full attention to their conversation.

"A man named New Hampshire (as you know, of course, all soldiers are called by the names of their native states) was holding forth on the subject of New Hampshire women. 'There's something about New Hampshire women,' said New Hampshire, 'some warmth, some inner fire.'

"'What about Wyoming women?' asked Wyoming.

"'They're all bowlegged from riding horses,' said Ohio.

"Wyoming countered with a utilitarian observation.

"And so it went, each man extolling the women of his own state, save Utah, whose silence was caused by his state's adherence to the horrendous practice of female infanticide. But even Utah, foiled on one count, put in a plug for the Great Salt Lake. Finally it grew late, and the sergeant, District of Columbia, came in and turned off the lights.

"I lay in the dark for a long time and pondered what I had

heard. Here were these young men about to go off perhaps to their deaths, and their thoughts were ever on the places of their births. How deep-rooted, how American. Here were men who clung to the real, simple things in these perilous times, who knew deeply and without being told what were the issues of the conflict. And here was I, still thinking in terms of hot-foots and Katzenjammer pranks, refined, to be sure, for with me it is a science.

"And all at once I knew that I had no right to be with them, to wear the same uniform as they did. I was not a soldier; I was a buffoon, an addlepate, an impostor. It was a hard thing to learn, Dan, hard.

"I resolved that night that I would henceforth change my ways. Instead of contributing to the mental anguish of the populace, I would turn into a living advertisement for Minnesota women. I too, by God, was a soldier."

"That's real nice, Sam," I said.

"So, you see, you no longer have anything to fear from me."

"I'm glad."

"I was hoping you would be," he said simply.

We drifted into shore. We threw the anchor up on the beach and carried the lunch out. There were sandwiches of salami, cheese, tongue, liver sausage, bologna, veal loaf, spiced ham, corned beef, and sardines. There were dill pickles, potato salad, relish, mustard, mayonnaise, green olives, ripe olives, and hard-boiled eggs. For dessert there was chocolate cake, fig bars, raisin cookies, candied apples, brown Betty, and éclairs.

"You know," said Sam as we ate with mess-hall delicacy, "it is an unending wonder to me how civilians have managed to subsist on wartime rations."

"In this total war," I said, "we must all make sacrifices."

"True," he agreed. "But privation rests lightly on our people."

"We are the stock of pioneers," I reminded him.

"Aye, a sturdy folk, fond of smörgåsbord and competitive sports," he said. "Minneapolis will hold out. I can see it in the faces of the people. 'War,' you say to them, and they answer, 'War?' and the air is rent by their full-throated laughter."

"To laugh is to win," I said.

"Indeed," Sam continued. "I have seen their faces. I have seen tall, loose-hung farmers at the teats of their milch kine and I have said to them, 'How now?' and they have answered, 'I milk that every Hottentot shall thrive, and to me parity is a word but partly understood, but I am a member of a nation at war, and come what may, I shall get fourteen cents a quart for my milk, which is three cents more than in the days of Calvin, the silent, than whom I thought there could be none better. You speak to me of Japanese on Pacific atolls, and I answer simply, 'I milk.''

"I have encountered tall, loose-hung arc welders, their eyes bulging appreciatively at the flamboyant pectorals of a feminine cartridge loader, and I have said, 'Say then,' and they have answered, 'For fifty minutes of each hour, which, you will agree, is a full five sixths, I fashion the instruments of retribution against those who have essayed to break our peace. For ten minutes of each hour I am allowed to relieve myself, a humane interval in years past when such functions did not require the aid of tobacco, but, you must agree, scarcely long enough now. I am paid again as much as I earned setting pins in a bowling alley, and when I properly learn this vexing craft of welding, I shall get even more. And when you speak to me of conflicts beyond the sea, I answer, "In my fashion, I weld."'

"I have spoken to tall, loose-hung brokers on the floor of the exchange, and I have said, 'What, sirs?' and they have answered, 'Wheat becomes flour, and corn becomes feed, and my commission remains constant and constantly increases as the prices of those things in which I deal increase. But the object, I recognize, is neither to fatten the hogs nor the populace (and my commissions are pleasant incidentals), but to win the struggle into which we have been plunged. The corrugated-iron sheds called ever-normal granaries, which were conceived by an ever-abnormal man, I say are vicious importations from Red Russia, our gallant ally. *Laissez faire* was good enough, etc., and by God, it's good enough for me. You speak to me of equitable distribution, and I say, "I sell grain."'"

"Try one of these low-calorie goose-liver sandwiches," I suggested.

Sam complied. "Yummy," he pronounced. "And I have spoken to tall, loose-hung dealers in foodstuffs, and I have said, 'Well, and——' and they have answered, 'Today I am told to sell for this and tomorrow for that, and price ceilings bob like a thing alive, and red and blue stamps haunt my dreams, and that is the cross I bear, who have been schooled in what the traffic will bear. My friends will sustain my contention that I am a reasonable man, and to me it appears more seemly that I know better what to sell and for how much, and let the so roundly discredited academicians in our nation's capital befog themselves with high-falutin theories and red and blue oblongs. If I have, I sell, cash, and carry, quick turnover, *caveat emptor*, and competitive bidding is the life of trade. You describe to me a hobgoblin called inflation, and I reply, "I am a grocer."'

"I have talked with tall, loose-hung industrialists, and I have said, 'I listen,' and they have answered, 'I converted from buggy whips to gun mounts when my own wife said I couldn't do it. I have slept tandem with total strangers in Washington while I was floating a million-dollar loan from the RFC, I, who two years ago employed a single employee named Olaf who stayed with me only because I knew he was wanted for sodomy in his native Lapland. I have solved the absentee problem by not taking attendance. An "E" pennant flutters atop my administration building. Contracts for shackle joints, nose fuses, ball turrets, .37-millimeter barrels, gear housings, sleeve bearings, and shell casings clog my files, I, whose very life is testimony to my belief in the evanescence of self-propelled vehicles. My secretary gets and earns $30,000 a year. I have not seen my wife since Christmas last. I am bound for Washington again next week to float another million-dollar loan, and I will get it. It would be idle to deny that my safety-deposit vault is gorged with currency, but that, by God, is mine. You speak to me of fox holes and pill-boxes, and I say, "I converted from buggy whips." '

"Yes," said Sam, "Minneapolis will hold out."

By now only two pieces of cake and two hard-boiled eggs remained. We made a sandwich of them, ate it, and fell insensible to the turf.

CHAPTER XI

THAT NIGHT we went to the Sty, a charming little tearoom on the edge of town run by a retired madame. Red, green, and yellow neon lights bathed the front of the place in a soft glow, and cheery signs blinked: "CHECKS CASHED," "BEST FLOOR SHOW IN TOWN," "OPEN ALL NIGHT," "DRINK OLD SPECIMEN," and "BUY BONDS." The proprietress, looking old-worldly in a red satin gown slit down one side to expose a flaccid thigh, bid us welcome at the door. "Just in time, gents," she said. "Floor show's just going on."

And indeed it was. We paid our three-dollar *couvert* and were relegated to a newly built, but as yet unenclosed, addition within artillery range of the dance floor. Renting binoculars from a cigarette girl in a rather daring costume (she was mother naked), we adjusted the lenses and watched the first number.

It was entitled simply "America." A line of lasses clad in red, white, and blue G-strings and a dab of phosphorus on each nipple advanced to the center of the floor, kicked once to the left, once to the right, about-faced, touched buttocks by pairs, about-faced, and screeched the following ditty:

"We are the Styettes.
We're here to entertain you;
We're here to entertain you.
We are the Styettes.

"Our country is at war with a treacherous foe.
We'll stick with our boys through thick and thin.
We'll give 'em hell, we'll make 'em yell, and soon they will know
That Uncle Sammy-Whammy's going to win.

"Guns and tanks and jeeps and ships and airplanes that fly
Will lick the dirty, rotten so-and-so.
On the land, on the sea, and up in the sky,
Come on, U.S.A., come on, we'll show
'Em.

"We are the Styettes.
We're here to entertain you;
We're here to entertain you.
We are the Styettes."

The Styettes waited for the laggards among them to finish, kicked once to the left, once to the right, about-faced, touched buttocks by pairs (a routine they knew consummately), and retired from the floor.

"By God," said Sam, "there's some music coming out of this war. That last was every bit as good as 'The Jap's a Sap; We'll Slap His Yap.'"

"Or 'Hiddler, the Piddler, Will Soon Play Second Fiddler,'" I added.

Now a pair of comics came out and rocked the joint with some snappy patter concerning a baseball game: "Who's on first base?" "No, Who's pitching. Why's on first base." "Why?" "Because he's the first baseman. What's on second base." "What?" "Yes," etc., etc.

We ordered drinks from a waiter who was about to get nasty

about it. "Can't live off'n people just settin' around," he chided gently as he brought our watered whisky and water.

Two ripe matrons came over to our table. The bolder one said, "We been watching you two soldiers, and we thought you might be lonesome, so we thought we'd join you if you don't mind."

"For patriotic reasons," said the other.

They sat down. "I'm Mrs. Spetalnik," said the first, "and this is my girl friend, Mrs. Gooberman."

"Blanche and Madge," supplied the second.

"Which is which?" asked Sam.

His little jest dispelled the formality, and we fast became friends. We ordered drinks, whisky for us, sloe-gin fizzes for the ladies. "I seldom ever drink," said Blanche, whom I had drawn. "It just helps sometimes to get away from the war. Know what I mean?"

"I understand," I said simply.

"What's your gentlemen's names?" asked Madge.

"Oh, excuse me," Sam said. "This is Robert Jordan, and I am Montag Fortz."

"Pleased, I'm sure," they said.

"I'll bet you gentlemen have seen plenty of action," Blanche said.

"I, nothing. But Robert——" said Sam. "Tell them of the bridge, Robert."

"The floor show," I said.

The m.c. was at the microphone calling for order. During the preceding number, a routine in which the Styettes wandered among the tables patting customers' heads, one of them had failed to return, and there was some confusion. At length the m.c. restored quiet. "And now, ladies and gentlemen," he said, "let's get serious for a moment. We're all having a lot of fun tonight, but our hearts are with the boys over there." A blue spot was thrown on him, and the pianist played soft chords. "Everybody here has got somebody near and dear to them over there," he continued. "Let's take time out for a minute and think of them. They haven't got it easy in the mud and filth of their fox holes. They never know when death will strike them, but they don't complain. They've got a job to do."

Blanche's hand stole into mine.

"We're all doing all we can on the home front." There was a round of applause. "But we must do even more, although it don't hardly seem possible. So tonight Miss Emma Fligg, proprietress of the Sty, has arranged a little added attraction."

Miss Fligg stuck her leg through the slit in her dress and bowed in acknowledgment of the ovation.

"Tonight," the m.c. went on, "we're all going to have a chance to make a further contribution toward speeding the day of victory. Come out, Miss Petite." Miss Petite came out. "Ladies and gentlemen, Dawn Petite!"

Dawn Petite was dressed in a costume of four strategically placed war bonds. "Who'll buy my bonds?" she asked.

"Yes, ladies and gentlemen," said the m.c., "who'll buy Miss Petite's bonds and win the privilege of taking them off? The first one goes for $18.75."

A large man in a black, pin-striped suit with a black shirt and a yellow tie rushed forward. He lunged at Miss Petite. "Whoa," chuckled the m.c. "Just a minute. What is your name, sir?"

"Ed Tarboosh," he said impatiently, and started for Miss Petite.

"And what is your occupation?"

"Riveter."

"Riveter!" cried the m.c.

The patrons stamped and whistled.

"I suppose you're working on war materials," said the m.c.

"Yeh, yeh."

"Well, Mr. Tarboosh, I want to say for everyone here that we're grateful to you home-front soldiers."

"The bond," said Mr. Tarboosh.

"All right. Now, Miss Petite, will you kindly turn around and let Mr. Tarboosh take his $18.75 bond?"

Although Mr. Tarboosh was more than a little disappointed, he made the best of it.

"The next two go for $37.50 apiece," said the m.c.

"I'll take 'em both," cried a slavering fellow running up with cupped hands.

"Your name, sir?"

"Hitler," he answered. "Everybody kids me about it. I don't think they should. I'm a good American."

"I should say you are, Mr. Hitler," said the announcer. "You're certainly showing the proper spirit tonight."

"I do my best," said Mr. Hitler.

Which he also did in collecting his bonds.

"The last bond goes for $75," said the m.c.

Instantly the place was in an uproar. From the melee one man finally reeled, his left arm hanging useless, a broken beer bottle in his right. He snarled at the m.c., knocked the microphone down, and went forward to claim his reward as the lights went off. When they went on again, Miss Petite was in her dressing room nursing a chill and the m.c. was imploring everyone out on the floor to dance.

"Tell us about the bridge," said Blanche to me.

"Would you care to gavotte?" I asked.

"You got to show me how," she said, taking my arm.

The dance floor was jammed with war workers and their wives, war workers and other men's wives, war workers' wives and other men, and war workers' wives dancing with war workers' wives. Blanche and I inserted ourselves into the mass and were there imbedded in erotic juxtaposition until the music stopped. We met Sam, who had also been dancing, as the impressions of his brass buttons on Madge's bare midriff testified, and we all went back to our table.

There were four strangers sitting at it, a pair of twin brothers and a pair of twin sisters. We looked at them askance. "Your table?" asked one of the brothers jovially. "Well, think nothing of it. Come on, Al, we'll get some more chairs." They reconnoitered briefly, unseated four near-by women, and came back in a moment with the chairs.

"Sit down, sit down," boomed the one who wasn't Al. "Plenty

of room. Glad to have you, soldiers. We've got a couple of twin brothers in the Army ourselves, haven't we, Al?"

"Yes," said Al.

We squeezed around what had been originally a tête-à-tête table.

"P.B. Gelt's my name," continued Al's brother, "and this is my brother Al. Used cars is our business. You've heard of Gelt and Gelt. 'If your last car smelt, try Gelt and Gelt.' And these are the Vanocki twins, Vera and Viola. Met 'em at the twins' convention in St. Paul last year. Damn fine girls."

They blushed in unison.

"Charmed," said Sam. "This is Madge Spetalnik and Blanche Gooberman and Robert Jordan and I am Montag Fortz."

"Well, that's fine," said P.B. "Waiter, eight shots of gin. Fortz, did you say your name was? I used to know a Fortz, didn't I, Al?"

"Yes," said Al.

"I remember now. Sold him a '27 Essex a couple of years ago. Had over 100,000 miles on it, two sprung axles, cracked block, and not an inch of wiring. He never even got it home," chuckled P.B. "No relation of yours, I hope."

"My father," said Sam. "He spent his last nickel for that car. My mother was selling shoelaces door to door at that time. She was out at a little settlement about thirty miles north of here when she was suddenly stricken with scrofula. The only chance was to get some serum to her immediately, and the only way to reach her was by car. Dad pawned everything he had in the world to buy that car. He didn't make it."

"Well, see here," said P.B., "I feel I ought to do something——"

"It doesn't matter," said Sam. "She was getting old anyway."

"It's nice of you to say so," said P.B. The waiter brought the drinks. "Eight more. By God, Fortz, you're not paying for a thing tonight. That's the least I can do."

"I'll bet you gentlemen have seen plenty of action," said Vera and Viola in unison.

"Robert has," said Blanche. "Tell them about the bridge, Robert."

"Mustn't let our drinks get cold," I said brightly.

We drank. "We've got a pair of twin brothers in the service," said P.B. "They're walkie-talkies."

"What about the bridge?" chorused Vera and Viola.

"Oh," I said, "I used to play a little bridge, that's all. Tell me, Mr. Gelt, how is the used-car business? I understand it's getting difficult to find good ones."

"Well," said P.B. pontifically, "it is and it isn't. You got to know where to find them. I got a '38 Olds on the lot—drive it away for $1,100, cash or terms—that's a little dandy. Just as good as brand new. Even better, 'cause it's been broke in. Used to belong to an old one-legged lady who just drove it back and forth in the garage for a few minutes every Sunday afternoon. Hardly a mile on the speedometer. Interested, Jordan? Might make a price for a serviceman."

"No," I said, "no, I don't think so. I was thinking of something bigger than an Olds. A Mercedes-Benz or a Rolls, perhaps."

"He got used to foreign cars while he was on the other side," Sam explained.

"Why don't you tell 'em about the bridge, hon?" asked Blanche.

"Well, look who's here!" I said. "The waiter! I certainly am glad to see you."

We drank, and P.B. ordered eight more. "By God, Fortz," he said, "I'm sorry about your mother."

"Forget it," said Sam. "She was a nuisance."

Blanche tugged at my sleeve. "Go on, tell 'em, Bob," she urged.

Miss Fligg was making the rounds of the tables. "Oh, Miss Fligg," I called. She came over. "I just wanted to tell you how much we're enjoying ourselves."

"That's real nice, dearie," she said. "I try to run a nice homey place where people can have a little fun and take their minds off this terrible war."

"Ain't it the truth?" Blanche agreed. "I seldom ever drink, but it helps sometimes to get away from the war, like you say."

The waiter brought the drinks. "Won't you have one?" I asked.

Miss Fligg laughed lightly. "No, thanks, dearie. Got to watch my figger." She exhibited her gnarled leg through the slit in her gown. "What you drinking, gin? Have you tried a Sty Stinger? Specialty of the house. One part rye, one part beer, and one part pure U.S.P. alky. Bring these folks a round of Sty Stingers," she told the waiter. "Well, folks, enjoy yourselfs. I got to go to the kitchen and watch the cook. That sonofabitch puts butter in the sandwiches when I ain't looking."

We drank the gin. The waiter brought the Sty Stingers and we drank those.

"How about the God-damn bridge?" asked Madge.

"Yes, tell us, Bobby," said Blanche.

"Yes, tell us about the bridge," said Vera and Viola together.

"We'd like to hear about it, Jordan," said P.B. "Wouldn't we, Al?"

"Yes," said Al.

"You tell them or I will," Sam threatened.

It was the Sty Stinger on top of the gin and whisky that did it. "Go obscenity thyself," I told Sam. "I will tell them. Who blew the bridge?"

"Thee," said Sam.

"Clearly," I said. "It was really nothing. Nada. A little bridge. A boy of twelve could have blown it."

"Thou art modest," said Sam. "It was a formidable bridge. The grandmother of all bridges. The Frank Sinatra of bridges."

"Was it a cantilever bridge or a suspension bridge?" asked P.B.

"What's the difference?" inquired Madge.

"A cantilever bridge is supported by spans," P.B. explained, "and a suspension bridge hangs from wires."

"Hangs from wires?" Madge asked. "Where do the wires come from?"

"From the wire factory," Sam said. "Tell them of the bridge, Roberto."

"That of the bridge fills me with sadness," I sighed. "I keep thinking of Anselmo."

"Who's Anselmo?" asked the twin sisters.

"Private First Class Herbert Anselmo," Sam said. "He helped Robert with the bridge. He was killed."

"Nevertheless, it was done," I said stoutly. "The Moors did not attack over *that* bridge."

"Where was the bridge?" Madge asked.

"Where do you suppose the Moors are?" asked P.B. irritably. "In Moorocco, naturally. Aren't they, Al?"

"Yes," said Al.

"Before I tell," I suggested, "let us have more of those drinks with the rare name."

"Eight Sty Stingers," P.B. told a waiter.

"A rare name," I said.

"Did you blow up the bridge?" Blanche asked.

"Did I not," I said. "I ask thee, Montag."

"Oh, did thee not," said Sam.

"Oh, did I not," I said.

The waiter brought another round. I drank mine, and Sam kindly gave me his, which I also drank.

"Tell them from the beginning," Sam said. "Tell them that of Maria."

"Who's Maria?" Blanche asked.

"She of the short hair like a cropped wheat field," I said dreamily.

"Who?" Blanche demanded.

"Maria Fashbinder," Sam explained. "A woman with a feather bob who was sent along to keep house for Robert."

"Maria," I breathed. "Ah, *guapa*. Ah, little rabbit."

"What?" said Blanche.

"He says for suppa they used to eat a little rabbit," Sam answered. "You get pretty tired of K ration."

"I can imagine," said Madge. "That kind of stuff ain't natural. One night Rex—Mr. Spetalnik—brought home a little package of green stuff. 'What's that?' I says. 'That's dehydrated spinach,' he says. 'They's a whole bushel here. All you got to do is add water.' 'Rex,' I says, 'if the Lord had intended for spinach to be like that, he would have grew it that way.' I divorced Rex shortly after that. Don't know how I stood him as long as I did. He used to work in the stockyards, and every night he came home with manure on his shoes. He tracked so much manure on the rugs things was growin' there. Believe me, you don't know what us women go through."

"Amen," said Blanche. "Gooberman used to keep bees in our dresser. I opened the wrong drawer one night, and they raised lumps all over me. I've still got some."

"Yes," said Al.

"What about the bridge?" asked Vera and Viola.

"A formidable bridge. The grandmother of all bridges," I said.

"Tell them how thou blewst it up after Pablo stole thy exploder," Sam prompted.

"Unprint him. I this and that on him. That he would steal a man's exploder."

"That's a shoddy thing to do," said P.B.

"It could have been done safely. There was no need for Anselmo to die," I complained softly.

"Tell them how thou climbst among the girders of the bridge and fastened grenades to the explosives," said Sam.

"I climbst among the girders of the bridge and fastened grenades to the explosives," I said.

A man materialized beside me. "Eight Sty Stingers," I said. "A rare name."

"I'm not a waiter," said the man. "I'm John Smith of the *Press-Telegram*. But I'll be glad to buy the drinks if I can hear the rest of that story."

"A reporter?" asked Sam.

"Well, sort of. I'm temporarily on classified ads," John Smith replied.

"A rare name," I said. "Even as I fixed the grenades to the explosives I could hear them coming up the road."

"Who?" asked John Smith.

"The fascists," Sam answered.

"How many of you were there?"

"Only he and Anselmo, who was killed," Sam said.

"And where was this bridge?"

"In Moorocco," said P.B. "Wasn't it, Al?"

"Yes," said Al.

"Maybe I better get a photographer," said John Smith.

"By all means," said Sam.

"Here's your drink," John Smith said to me. "Now you drink this and I'll be right back. Wait for me."

He got back as I finished the Sty Stinger. A rare name. "Now let me have your name and address," he said.

"I'll give you all that later," said Sam. "Let him go ahead with his story. You got pencil and paper, Mr. Smith?"

"Shoot," he said.

I continued. "I could hear them coming up the road. 'Thee must pull the wire, Anselmo,' I said, 'if they reach the bridge.' 'Nay,' he said, 'not while thou arst on it.' 'It is of no consequence,' I said. 'Thee must pull the wire.'"

"Jeez, what a story!" exclaimed John Smith. "They can't keep me on classified ads after this one."

"She came to me as I lay in the sleeping bag," I said. "'Get in, little rabbit,' I said. 'Nay, I must not,' she said. 'Get in. It is cold out there,' I said. 'Thee must show me what to do,' she said. 'I will learn and I will be thy woman.' 'Yes,' I said fiercely, 'yes, yes.'"

"What's all this?" asked John Smith.

"Nay," said Sam. "Tell them of the bridge. How thou hadst finished one side and they were coming and thou strungst the wire down the other side and they started to fire and thou finished the other side just as they reached the bridge and thou saidst, 'Pull, Anselmo,' and he pulled and the bridge opened up just like a blossom."

"Did it not," I said. "A formidable bridge."

"This story will make me," said John Smith excitedly. "Waiter, a round of drinks for everyone."

"P.B. Gelt's my name," said P.B. Gelt. "I imagine a newspaperman like you needs a good car in his business, doesn't he, Al?"

"Yes," said Al.

"They're getting scarce. You could do worse than invest in a good car a few years old. They knew how to build cars in those days, believe me. Now I got a '27 Essex——"

"Here's my photographer," said John Smith.

"Of course, if you'd like something a little newer," said P.B., "I got a '38 Olds—$1,300 takes it, cash or terms—that used to belong to a paralyzed clergyman who just went out and sat in it on warm afternoons. Never even started the motor."

"Manny," said John Smith to the photographer, "I want to get something a little unusual here. This guy blew up a bridge in Morocco. The fascist troops were shooting at him while he attached the explosives. They got his buddy."

"The bastards," said Manny.

"What do you think?" asked John Smith.

"Well, we'll fake something," said Manny. He turned to me. "You crawl under the table and I'll give you this extension wire and you pretend you're hooking it onto the table leg. You, the other soldier—what's your name?"

"Montag Fortz."

"—stand by with your fingers in your ears."

"Swell," said John Smith. "I won't be writing classified ads much longer."

"Thee," Sam said to me, "getst under the table."

I crawled under. "I had a cousin who was a photographer," I said. "He smuggled a camera into an electrocution once. Had it strapped to his leg. When they turned the juice on the prisoner, my cousin hoisted his trousers and clicked the shutter.

Unfortunately, he wasn't able to focus. All he got was the nape of H. V. Kaltenborn, who was covering the electrocution for the Brooklyn *Eagle*. Kaltenborn later bought a dozen enlargements from him."

"All right," Manny said. "Now tie that wire around the table leg. That's it. Montag, you stick your fingers in your ears. That's fine. Now one more. Got it."

"Now, if you'll give me the dope on your friend——" John Smith said to Sam.

Sam took him aside.

"Gelt and Gelt," I said from under the table, "I see what you're doing to those twins. A rare thing."

CHAPTER XII

"We've had a fine day," said Sam.

We were sitting in the car in front of Sam's house. "A rare day," I agreed.

"How do you feel now?" he asked.

"All right now, I guess."

"Do you remember running over those four children on the way home?"

"Five, wasn't it?"

"No. The fifth was their father. A midget. He works for Philip Morris."

"What became of those two bags we had?"

"We took them home. Don't you remember? You gave them all the fish we caught this morning."

"Did I? That was nice of me."

"Oh, I wouldn't say that. You made them sit up and bark like seals, and then you threw them the fish one at a time."

"Oh, Jesus, did I really?"

"Did you? It's a good thing that cop had a sense of humor."

"What cop?"

"The one you asked why he wasn't in uniform. Say, how much do you remember about tonight?"

"Well, after that first Sty Stinger——"

"A rare name."

"—everything goes sort of hazy."

"You don't remember going to Estherlee McCracken's house?"

"Oh, my God. What did I do there?"

"Not much, fortunately. I wouldn't let you ring the bell. But you insisted on leaving your card in the mailbox."

"Well, that wasn't so bad."

"The card, no. But it was in a crappie's mouth."

"Sam, is there any chance of me shipping out with you?"

"Buck up, Roberto. There's always the river."

"Yeah, the river. That reminds me. I vaguely recall something about a bridge. Some involved story. What was that?"

"Bridge? I don't remember any bridge. But you bought a '38 Olds from the Gelt brothers."

"Now I know you're lying. Where did I get the money?"

"When you picked that guy's pocket on the dance floor."

"You bastard. The truth isn't in you."

"You bought yourself a fine automobile. Not a mile on it. The guy that owned it was president of a suicide-pact club. He used to keep the car in the garage, and once a month one member of the club would go out and monoxide himself. That's all the car was used for."

"Sometimes people say to me, 'Is Sam Wye a friend of yours?' and I unthinkingly answer yes."

"That's a fine way to talk to a comrade in arms who is leaving for the wars in a couple of days."

"Where are they sending you, Sam?"

"I don't know."

"What are you going to do?"

"Kill people."

I looked at my watch. "It's almost five. I better let you get some sleep."

"Yeah, I guess so. Well, it's been a fine day, Roberto."

"Yes. Good night, Sam."

"Good night, Dan. I'll see you in the papers."

Little did I know.

CHAPTER XIII

I OPENED ONE EYE, looked about me, and idly wondered how come Olsen and Johnson had picked my bedroom to put on a show. I closed the eye gingerly.

"He's up!" The cry rose from a thousand throats.

This time I sat straight up, both eyes wide open. A circle of huge, pulsing faces moved in on me. Feverishly I seized the water bottle on my night table, filled a glass, drank thirstily, filled and drank several times more. Later I learned that the water bottle had been empty all the time.

"Now then," I squeaked sternly, "what does all this mean?"

Mama, as was her due, had the first go at me. "My baby!" she cried. "My hero!" She clasped me to her bosom and sobbed mightily down the back of my Fo-To-Mon-Taj-Ies, causing the Eiffel Tower to run into the second Louis-Schmeling fight.

Next came Papa, who pulled my hand out of the sleeve of my pajamas, where it had retreated in alarm, and wrung it robustly. "I'm proud of you, Son," he said. "Proud."

He was followed by Estherlee, who was wearing a low-neck-lined dress. She bent over, nudged me softly in the chin, and kissed my forehead. "I've been such a fool," she said.

77

She was replaced by a vaguely familiar young man. "You remember me. I'm John Smith. *Press-Telegram* reporter. Yes sir. Reporter. No more of those damn classifieds. 'Wanted. Grl fr genl hswk. No wshg. No chldn. Thurs, Sun off. Opprtnty fr advcmt.' Yes sir. Reporter."

It was Mama's turn again. "No wonder you are so skinny. How can you get fat blowing up bridges?" she wailed.

"Later," said Papa, "we'll look at the map, and I'll show you where you did it. I've got a brand-new map. The whole world fits into your vest pocket. Here, I'll show you." He pulled a small folded paper from his vest pocket. "See," he said. "Like I said, the vest pocket. Now you take this end and I'll unfold it." He shoved the corner of the map into my unresisting hand and started to unfold the map. He walked backward as he unfolded, out the bedroom door, through the upstairs hall, and down the stairs.

"Can you ever forgive me?" said Estherlee, swinging low again.

"I want you to meet two men whom you will get to know very well in the next few days," said John Smith. "This is the *Press-Telegram's* military analyst, Colonel Cosmo Fairfax Swatch——"

An elderly character with side whiskers and a modified sombrero whacked me over the patella with a gnarled walking stick. "Well done, Sergeant," he pronounced. "Reminds me of a time with the 214th Light Horse—or was it the 48th Grenadiers?—no —yes. Let me see." He pondered for a moment, then walked over to Estherlee and pinched her arm. "Ziggetty!" he said.

"—and O. Merriam Phyfe," said John Smith.

"I speak for His Honor Mayor La Hoont and all of Minneapolis," sleek, sonorous O. Merriam Phyfe said, "when I say that we're proud of you."

"Oklahoma, Oklahoma. All the time he told us he was in Oklahoma," Mama complained bitterly.

"He didn't want to worry you, Mrs. Miller—Mother," Estherlee said.

Colonel Swatch suddenly walked over to the picture of the Indian on my wall and smashed it with his walking stick. "Damn redskins," he spat. "They killed George."

"George who?" I screamed in sheer desperation.

"George Custer." He resumed pinching Estherlee. "Fat women," he said. "Zum."

"Can you hear me?" came Papa's faint voice from outside. "I'm on the front lawn. Still unfolding."

"I'm public relations counsel to His Honor Mayor La Hoont," O. Merriam Phyfe confessed.

"Is it any wonder that I am gray, my hair?" Mama asked.

John Smith took a newspaper from his pocket. "I don't suppose you've seen it yet. Rather unusual story. Yes. Quite unusual. All in free verse. Had the devil's own time persuading the city editor to run it. Heh, heh."

"It's too bad you'll be here such a short time," said O. Merriam Phyfe. "Well, no matter. We'll make the best of it."

"I didn't realize what a lucky girl I was," whispered Estherlee. "But I know now." She turned angrily on Colonel Swatch. "Will you stop?" she demanded.

There was a sudden shriek outside. Mama ran to the window. "What's the matter?"

"I unfolded all the way across the street," yelled Papa. "Then a bus went by."

"In view of the subject matter," said John Smith, "I thought that free verse would be the only proper medium. Except, of course, an epic poem, but the haste incident to publication rather precludes an epic, don't you think?"

"Naturally we'd like to plan a fuller program," said Phyfe. "As it is, we can only hit the high spots. Now, first——"

"I think Sergeant Miller would like to hear the story," John Smith interrupted with injured dignity.

"Of course," said O. Merriam graciously.

"Me?" cried Mama, pushing Colonel Swatch away. "An old woman? A mother of children?"

"I'll read it now, if nobody objects," said John Smith.
There were no objections. He began:

"By John Smith

*"I met an ordinary young man last night who had done an
      extraordinary thing.*
Daniel Miller is his ordinary name.
Sergeant is his ordinary rank.
Mr. and Mrs. Adam Miller are his ordinary parents.
They live in an ordinary house at 2123 Fremont Avenue.
An ordinary street.

"Perhaps the thing he did was not extraordinary.
He risked his life to save his country.
Perhaps we all would.
Would you? Would I?
If we all would, it is not extraordinary
But ordinary.

"He did this thing, ordinary or extraordinary, in a far place.
A place whose very name means romance to most of us.
Morocco.
It did not mean romance to him.
It meant danger, death, dust, destruction.
And chow.
Chow for breakfast, chow for lunch, chow for dinner.
Chow, chow, chow.

"A bridge can be a friend.
To take you over a river where ford there is none.
To speed you home to those you love.
A bridge can be a friend.

"A bridge can be an enemy.
It was in Morocco.
*In Morocco a bridge was a dagger in the back of American
      boys,*

*Boys from Iowa and Connecticut and Utah and all forty-eight
    and the District of Columbia, ten square miles where the
    destinies of millions are ruled.*
*Beyond the bridge were the fascists, teeth bared, poised to
    plunge into the American flank.*
The bridge was the enemy, the spoiler of progress and time.
The bridge held up the offensive.
Men and guns languished.

"The bridge was the enemy and it had to be destroyed.
Sergeant Miller was sent to destroy it.
Another accompanied him, Private First Class Herbert An-
    selmo, whom they killed.
The bastards.
Together these two destroyed the bridge.
That is the thing that Daniel Miller did.
That is his story.

"He did not want to tell me his story.
He is shy. It becomes a hero to be shy.
A friend prompted, wheedled, cajoled—in fact told most of
    the story.
The name of the friend is Montag Fortz.
An ordinary name.

"To destroy the bridge would have been a simple task (They
    call these things simple. Let you or I destroy a bridge.)
    had not Miller's exploder been stolen by a native.
A malicious thing done without malice.
A native is a child.
This native, whose name was Pablo, had a hobby of collecting
    exploders.
Miller's exploder, a new type called the Little Dandy Bang-
    Bang, appealed to Pablo.
So he stole it.
This Fortz explained.

"*The bridge had to be exploded with grenades.*
Grenades had to be lashed to the bridge's supports and wires had to be fastened to the grenades.
When the wires were pulled, the grenades would explode and collapse the bridge.
Ingenious?
American.

"*Miller lashed the grenades.*
Anselmo held the wires.
Two Americans at work.
With nothing to eat but chow.

"*Then the fascists came.*
Miller was not half through.
He knew he must finish. He told Anselmo to pull if they reached the bridge before he was through.
'*No,*' *said Anselmo.*
'*Pull,*' *said Miller.*
'*No,*' *said Anselmo.*
'*Pull,*' *said Miller.*

"*Bullets crashed around Miller, a locusts' plague of steel.*
The thundering hooves of the enemy's tanks were on the bridge's approaches. Now they were on the edge of the bridge.
Miller finished.
'*Pull,*' *he said.*
Anselmo pulled his last pull.
They got him.
The bastards.

"*Miller came back.*
He is home now in Minneapolis.
An ordinary man in an ordinary city who did a thing that is perhaps extraordinary."

"My God," I gasped.

"Of course," said John Smith, "free verse in a news story is a little unusual, you might say, but, considering the subject matter, I thought it rather apropos."

Mama burst into tears and Estherlee took her into her arms, murmuring, "There, there, Mother."

"Two at once," said Colonel Swatch, closing a pincers on their flanks.

Papa came into the room looking disconsolate. "I could have unfolded for another half a block," he complained.

"There's a picture, too," said John Smith, handing me the paper. I took it in my trembling fingers and stared transfixed at a six-column picture of me lying under a table with a wire in my hand while Sam Wye stood by, unrecognizable, with his eyes closed, his front teeth clamped together, and his fingers in his ears.

"Now, then," said O. Merriam Phyfe, "here's what we have planned. First you'll address the Ladies Hearth and Hauteur Sodality. That's tomorrow night."

I tried to say no, but nothing came out.

"A fine group of women, the Hearth and Hauteur," he said. "His Honor Mayor La Hoont's wife is chairwoman."

"You must be starved," said Mama.

"You'll just speak for a half hour or so," continued Phyfe. "You won't have to prepare anything. Simply tell the ladies how they can further aid the war effort. Not that they're not doing a great deal now. His Honor Mayor La Hoont's wife has given a complete shelf of Gene Stratton Porter to the Army herself. Bound in limp leather. But these ladies want to do even more."

"I had a woman back in '07 weighed three hundred pounds," said Colonel Swatch, belaboring Estherlee's arm. "Fat. Zut! Squeeze her anywhere. She dropped dead the night of Halley's comet. Excitement, I guess. All six pallbearers got the hernia."

"It took me quite a while to decide that writing was my field," John Smith admitted. "I also paint and compose music. Do fine needlework too. I won first prize in a national Lutheran junior-college competition with an abstract painting of mine." He chuckled. "I'll bet they wouldn't have given it to me if they'd known it was a phallic symbol."

"And then," Phyfe resumed, "Colonel Swatch is going to interview you on his radio program 'Behind the Background of the News.' You've heard the program, of course."

"I listen to you every day, Colonel," said Papa. "I certainly liked your broadcast on Panzer warfare."

"Damn tanks," said the colonel. "In my day we didn't need 'em. Best thing the Army ever did was to organize anti-tank divisions. They probably got plenty of volunteers. Must be thousands of people against tanks. Good thing the Army gave 'em an opportunity to band together. There'll be excellent morale in those anti-tank companies—group of men bound together by a mutual dislike of tanks."

"Then we're constructing a recruiting booth for you downtown. You'll spend a day there helping young men about to enter the service decide on which branch to go into. It's quite a problem, you know. My own son, La Hoont, is seventeen now. He'll be going soon. He's having a devil of a time trying to decide whether to go right into Officer's Candidate School or spend some time in the ranks—to get better acquainted with the men, you know."

"I'm not angry you didn't tell me," said Estherlee. "In fact, I think even more of you."

"As for music," John Smith put in, "I've written one or two things. I wrote our class song the year we graduated junior college—'We've Got to Leave You, Alma Mater, and It's Hard.'"

"That was the last folding map they had," Papa mourned. "God knows when they'll get another."

"On Saturday the Minneapolis baseball club opens its season," O. Merriam Phyfe revealed. "I've arranged for you to pitch the first ball. I tried to get the newsreel men to be there, but they'll be busy covering a jeep demonstration that day."

"Tonight, dear," whispered Estherlee, "we'll go canoeing. Just you and I alone. Ooo!"

"Dinner will be ready in a little while," Mama said. "We'll all go down and eat if you don't mind potluck."

"Not I, madam," said the colonel. "I lived half a winter on buffalo chips once when I was chasing Geronimo. I never did get him. I got involved with a 110-pound woman who had a herd of white-faced cattle on a ranch outside Colorado Springs. I spent the rest of that winter trying to fatten her up. Slaughtered every last one of those cattle and fed 'em to her. Then in spring she got distemper and died. Can't trust a thin woman."

"For the grand finale," said Phyfe, "you are going to be the feature attraction at the dedication of the new war plant just built outside Minneapolis. This plant will be the world's largest producer of small-bore ammunition, and it's entirely His Honor Mayor La Hoont's doing. He saw the need for the factory, and he didn't ask anybody. He just went ahead and built it. He brushed aside all timid arguments. 'War Department approval?' he said. 'We'll get that later. What'll we make ammunition out of?' he said. 'We'll get steel from Pittsburgh and powder from Delaware and coal from Arkansas. This is total war!'"

"Honest to God," said Papa, "I should sue the bus company."

"His Honor Mayor La Hoont," continued Phyfe, "knows how eager our people are. Let me give you an example of the spirit of our Minnesotans. Two brothers, Egmont and Singletax Snide, one sixty-nine and the other eighty-one, used to build boats before the war on Lake Malchamovess, about one hundred and twenty miles north of here. When the war came these two old men decided to convert to war production. Inside of six months, without telling anyone, mind you, they build eight submarines. When the Navy heard about it a high-ranking admiral said that they were 'surprised and pleased.' Today a navy 'E' pennant floats over the Snides' humble lakeside boatworks. And when a way is figured out to get the Snide brothers' submarines to the sea, the Japs will soon learn the meaning of Minnesota patriotism."

"There'll be a full moon tonight," breathed Estherlee. "It said so in the paper."

"Naturally," Phyfe continued, "the dedication of the ammunition plant will be a gala occasion. His Honor Mayor La Hoont will be there himself. There'll be all sorts of notable people and festivities galore. You may well be proud, young man, that you've been chosen to be the feature attraction.

"And now I'll tell you about the climax. The construction of the plant is complete, but there still is one more thing to do. There is a dried-up river bed in front of the plant. While construction was going on, a makeshift wooden bridge was thrown over the river bed to allow workers to cross to the plant. But now that the factory goes into full operation, the wooden bridge will no longer be adequate. It will be replaced by a permanent steel-and-concrete bridge.

"This is where you come in. With your experience, of course, it will be very simple. As the highlight of the dedication ceremony, you are going to blow up the old bridge to make way for the new one."

I must have fainted, because the next thing I knew Mama was forcing a salami sandwich down my throat.

"No!" I bellowed. "No! The whole thing, no!"

They all drew back aghast.

"Dan," said Papa, "what's the matter with you? What are you saying?"

"He's hungry, that's all. He's out of his head from hunger," Mama offered.

"I'm not hungry. I'm in my right mind. I absolutely refuse to do the whole thing. All of it. Any of it."

"Darling," said Estherlee not too sweetly, "you've been modest up to now, and that was admirable. But now that your secret is out, there is no more need for modesty. After all, I want everybody to be as proud of you as I am."

"No."

"See here, Miller," said Phyfe sharply, "I and His Honor

Mayor La Hoont have gone to considerable trouble to plan these appearances. You can't just say no."

"I'm saying it."

"But it's all going to be in the paper," said John Smith. "The paper will be on the streets in another hour. I wrote a long story about it. In free verse."

"No."

"I'll be back on classified ads," wailed John Smith.

"Insubordination," Colonel Swatch hollered, pounding the floor with his walking stick. "Rank insubordination."

I shook my head stubbornly as they all talked at once.

"Wait a minute," said O. Merriam Phyfe. "Let me put it to him in another way. You may feel that you don't have to do any more than what you did in the line of duty. You may think that because you're in uniform you have no obligation to us civilians. Well, let me tell you, I'd give anything if I could join up, if I weren't tied down in this essential work for His Honor Mayor La Hoont."

"If I hadn't broken my arches doing an *entrechat* in the ballet at junior college, I'd be in myself," said John Smith.

"I've been waiting for them to come to their senses in Washington and put me back on the active list," thundered Colonel Swatch. "I'm tough. Many's the winter I've lived on buffalo chips and white-faced cattle."

"Say," said Papa, "maybe you think I wouldn't like to be in?"

"There you are," said Phyfe triumphantly. "We'd all like to be in service. I'm essentially employed, Mr. Smith is physically unfit, Colonel Swatch is past the retirement age, and I'm sure your father has some good reason for not being in uniform.

"But we hide our disappointment. We go on with our work. And our work, in its way, is as vital to the war effort as blowing up bridges. I help carry on government without which the state would crumble. Mr. Smith keeps the people informed. Colonel Swatch interprets the progress of the war. Your father does whatever it is he does.

"This is a total war, young man, as His Honor Mayor La Hoont often says. Each of us is a soldier. It isn't easy for us at home, wanting all the time to be over there but forced to stay here and contend with the inconveniences of war on the home front—no gas, no tires, no steaks, no butter. Rising prices and dwindling supplies. And all the time the heartbreak of not being able to be in uniform. As all soldiers do, we simply make the best of things.

"So when I ask you to make these appearances, it isn't just for the amusement of civilians. It's for the morale of an army! A home-front army!"

Papa, Colonel Swatch, and John Smith shook Phyfe's hand silently.

Estherlee laid wet eyes on my cheek. Her arms around me were very soft and very smooth. The neckline on her dress was low. "You will, won't you, darling?" she whispered.

I collapsed miserably in my pillows.

"He will," she told everybody.

"All right," said Mama briskly. "Everybody downstairs for dinner. Dan, you get dressed and come down right away. Look how pale he is. He's starving."

Glumly I watched them file out. Estherlee fended off Colonel Swatch with one hand and threw me a kiss with the other. "To-night," she called. "Canoeing. Full moon. Oooo."

As the door closed behind them I heard hoots of laughter out-side my window and I saw Sam Wye hanging on the trellis. "I thought sure they'd see me when your father started unfolding that map," he said, leaping into the room.

We discussed my plight as I chased him around the bed with a trench knife. "This should be a lesson to you, Roberto," he said. "Remember what Ben Franklin said: 'The truth stands on two legs, a lie on one.' Remarkable chap, Franklin. Had literally dozens of illegitimate children. 'Old Lightning Rod' they called him.

"But this is no time to be moralizing. I've got to help you out of the mess you got yourself into."

I growled throatily.

"No, don't thank me," said he. "My contribution will only be a small one. You've got to handle the women's club, the radio address, the recruiting booth, and the baseball game by yourself. I'll give you some assistance with blowing the bridge. Naturally I can't be present at the bridge blowing itself, because I'm shipping out in two days. But I can teach you sufficient demolition before I leave.

"Now, let's see. We'll have to practice at night. Tonight you're going canoeing with Estherlee. Good night for it, too. Full moon. We'll practice tomorrow night. All right?"

"You bastard," I snarled, and increased my speed.

"With luck," he continued, "you should be able to bluff this business out. In any case, you have no choice. If you spill the beans now, it's Leavenworth. The Army, I'm told, gets pretty upset about soldiers posing as heroes."

I stopped. "Surely," I cried, "you're not suggesting that I go through with this thing?"

"I can remember when you had a head on your shoulders," he answered. "What else can you do? Look at it logically. Two courses are open to you: one, you can bluff the whole business out on the very real chance that they'll never hear about it in Oklahoma, and two, you can make a full confession now and stand court-martial and make complete fools of your family.

"And then there's Estherlee. You've got her back now. Do you want to lose her again, lose her forever this time? Can you honestly face the prospect of no more Estherlee? Round, soft, supple Estherlee."

"You cut out talking like that. You know what it does to me."

"Smooth, fragrant, pneumatic Estherlee. The Earth Mother."

"But," I wailed, "they'll catch me anyhow, and it will go a lot harder."

"You're the kind of guy who carries an umbrella on sunny days. Isn't it worth taking a chance—and by no means a long chance—for Estherlee? So succulent, so resilient, so *female*."

I sat down on the bed. "Sam, don't lie to me. Can you really teach me demolition in one night?"

He slapped me on the back. "That's the big boy, Roberto. I knew you'd come to your senses."

Then he looked at his watch and with a cry of "Buy bonds" leaped out the window and was gone.

CHAPTER XIV

ONE EVENING in late August 1823, according to a 75-page history of Minnesota compiled in 1937 by 30,000 men and women on a WPA writers' project, a canoe stopped by the banks of the Mississippi where Minneapolis now stands. Three people got out—Otto de Fe, a trapper from Shreveport, Louisiana, his wife Euthanasia, and their fourteen-year-old boy, Emmett. They had left Shreveport several weeks before to visit kin in Covington, Kentucky, but had neglected to make a right turn at Cairo, Illinois, and had thus ended up in Minnesota. Otto, with masculine stubbornness, insisted all the way that he knew the river like a book and they could momently expect to run into a cutoff that would take them directly into the heart of Covington's business section (the Casbah). After several days, however, he yielded to his wife's whining and his son's accusing stares and stopped in Minnesota to ask directions of a group of Indians on the shore. The Indians promptly scalped Otto and Euthanasia. Emmett, who was somewhat hydrocephalic, they took back to the camp for laughs.

In the following weeks Emmett won the affection of the tribe, and they allowed him to roam at will within the radius of the 120-foot rope by which he was tied to a tent post. Near the end of September the men of the tribe set out for the Dakotas to hunt bison. Emmett, pleading a sick headache, stayed behind with the women. One night when the women were all up in the trees for a better view of an early manifestation of Halley's comet, Emmett seized his chance and escaped.

He plunged into the thick forest west of the river and ran until he reached a lake several miles away. Here he knelt and drank thirstily. He slept there that night, thinking to move on in the morning, but when he awoke, the serenity of his surroundings, the lush grass, the cool trees, the near, sweet water, made him loath to leave. The long blue lake dotted with many green islands promised haven and security. "Lake of the Isles," he said, "here I am and here I will stay."

He stayed there for many moons. The Indians came looking for him a few times, but he concealed himself well in evergreen thickets along the shore. At length they stopped coming. Emmett knew then that he was safe if he did not stray from Lake of the Isles, and he was well content to stay there.

The winter passed and spring came, and Emmett observed the birds and beasts about him and, without precisely comprehending, was moved to a condition of mysteriously acute longing. His needs, which in that spring of his fifteenth year daily became more persistent, were presently fulfilled. A girl named Griselda, herself in her fifteenth year, came into his camp, a truly amazing coincidence.

Griselda was Emmett's blood cousin, although neither ever knew it. She was one of the relatives in Covington, Kentucky, whom he and his family were on the way to visit when they got lost. Griselda's father, Minor Clendenning, had become worried when Emmett's family had not arrived in Covington. He waited a week or two and then sent a dispatch rider to Shreveport to find out whether they had left. The dispatch rider found out from their neighbor, an early linotypist named Schnecken, that they had left weeks ago. He returned the intelligence to Clendenning.

"Something must have happened," said Clendenning. "I think I'll mosey down the river and see what I can find out."

"Take me with, Pa," entreated Griselda, who was a great one for gadding about.

"No," said Clendenning. "The last time I took you down the river you ran off with a peddler."

"Take me, Pa," she pleaded. "I won't do anything this time."

The hell she didn't. When her father left her in the boat at Cairo, Illinois, while he went about to make inquiries, she immediately ran off with a fur trader named Harold Swebb. They went up the Mississippi to Minnesota, and life was satisfactory enough for Griselda. But in Minnesota he suddenly became all business. Instead of passionate overtures, he gave her otter pelts to clean. At night he spurned her, telling her to go away, she smelled gamy. She stood all she could and then left. That is how she came upon Emmett.

Emmett and Griselda were very happy for a few months with their idyl on the banks of Lake of the Isles. But as summer drew to an end, things began to pall on fun-loving Griselda. One night as they sat on the shore, their feet dangling into the water (Emmett's second greatest pleasure), she complained, "My God, ain't we ever gonna leave this place? I ain't seen another living soul in months."

But Emmett, who cared not at all for venturing out and getting caught by the Indians, answered, "Patience, my own. There'll come a day when many canoes will pass on Lake of the Isles."

How prophetic he was. That night when Estherlee and I went canoeing you could have walked across Lake of the Isles on the tops of canoes. The dark shores that had given Emmett refuge provided a superb setting for the activities of young lovers. The lake was long, and except on Saturdays and the nights before holidays, there was plenty of room for all. We sat patiently until the canoe jam dispersed toward the shores, and then I paddled out to the far end of the lake.

Estherlee trailed her hand in the water as we glided along.

"See, darling," she said, "a full moon. Just as it said in the paper."

"You mustn't place too much faith on things you see in the paper," I said.

She laughed lightly at what she assumed was a joke. She had changed her disturbing dress of that afternoon for a white linen sports dress, this one not cut so low but even more enticing in the perverse manner of women's clothes. She wore no stockings, and her soft white toes stuck out through open-toed sandals. (Is there something wrong with me? Toes excite me.) She leaned back easily on the cushions in the prow, her white arms resting gleamingly on the gunwales. I reached the shore at the end of the lake, and after a brief tussle with my animal self I turned the boat around and headed back. This was no time to get further wrapped up in my tissue of lies.

"Dan," said she, surprised, "why are we going back?"

"I've been waiting so long to get my hand on a paddle that I just want to row and row," I answered.

"I know, darling," she said, "out there in the desert you must have been simply mad to get back on a lake again."

"Yes," I said, not pleased.

"Sweetheart, would you like to tell me about it? About the bridge and everything? It might help if you told somebody."

"No, Estherlee, I'd rather not."

"I understand, dear. You don't have to talk about it unless you want to."

"Thank you," I said simply.

I paddled on past the sounds of face slapping and giggling along the shore. Estherlee smiled. "You can't blame them on a beautiful night like this, can you? I can't."

"This canoe sure is yare," I said.

"I love the way you handle a canoe. I love the way you do everything—the way you walk and talk and dance and move. In fact, I love you."

I almost lost the paddle.

"I've never stopped loving you since that night when—that night. When I broke with you, it was just because I loved you.

Can you understand that? It was you I loved, the real you, the fine man who left me last year to do whatever was necessary to save his country." She lowered her eyes. "The man for whom I did everything I could." She took a deep breath. "The man for whom I would do the same thing again."

The paddle did not fall into the water. It jumped halfway across the lake. "Oops," I said foolishly. Luckily there was a spare. I took a good interlocking grip on this one.

"Naturally, my sweet," she continued, "I understand what you did when you told me you were in Oklahoma. It was a magnificent thing. Because you are so modest and because you didn't want me to worry, you told me that you were safe and sound. You created another, a false, Daniel Miller for me. But don't you see, precious, the false Daniel Miller was a man whom I could not love? He was a despicable creature—sitting there in a sheltered office while others were dying for his cause. I could never love a man like that."

"Office workers," I piped, "are very essential in this war. You don't know how much paper work is necessary——"

"Dan," she interrupted, "you are so kind and generous that you think the best of everybody."

"—how much detail and tabulation must be gone through before any fighting units——"

"It's so like you to have kind words for men who were sitting in perfect safety while you risked your life fighting their war."

"—can reach the front. Records, data, filing systems are what keep the Army from being a——"

"I don't see how they dare wear the same uniforms as men who fight."

"—disorganized mob. The whole machine would bog down, collapse, if it weren't for the——"

"I just seethe inside when I think of all the men holding down soft jobs while you dodge bullets."

"—desk soldiers. Let me tell you about logistics. That's the science of moving troops and——"

"Naturally I understand that they must stay in this country

until they are trained, but after that, let them fight their war."

"—supplies to the places where they are needed. It's a fantastically big job." I finished rapidly while she lit a cigarette. "The men who run the war must have records, statistics, papers in order to know where and how much to send. Records of the disposition of all troops and all supplies must be in front of the generals before they can make a move. Without the records, costly blunders could be committed, lives could be needlessly lost. The man who keeps the generals informed is doing an indispensable job. Records, as much as bullets, are weapons."

We were at the other end of the lake. "Dear," she said, "have you paddled all you want now?"

"Huh? Oh no. Not yet. I think I'll go back to the other end again."

"Dan, you're not angry with me for the way I've acted?"

"Oh no. Not a bit."

"You're sweet. I thought maybe you might be because you won't stop paddling."

"No. It just feels so good to get a paddle in my hands again."

"I'd like to get *you* in my hands again," she said. She stretched out her arms and smiled. Her toes curled.

"Dear," I said thickly, "would you mind putting something over your toes?"

"I knew I shouldn't have worn open-toed shoes. I have such ugly old toes." She took off her shoes, lifted her legs, and wiggled her toes. "Such ugly old toes. But you'll have to take them, darling. They're part of me, and I'm all yours."

The second paddle went into the drink.

There was nothing I could do now as the tide washed the boat inexorably in to the shore. "Come sit next to me, sweet," she said.

"Is there room?"

"There always has been, hasn't there? Oh, I know I've gotten terribly fat."

"I wouldn't say that," I said truthfully as I moved into the cushions beside her.

"What would you say?"

"I'd say let's have a cigarette," I said brightly.

"I just threw one away, dear."

"Do you mind if I have one?"

"Of course. How thoughtless of me. You'll have to teach me to be considerate, darling. You'll have to teach me a lot of things. I've treated you so shoddily. Can you ever forgive me?"

"Estherlee," I said stoutly, "I believe in forgive and forget. With all my heart I do. I believe that when two people are in love she can forgive him anything. Anything at all. That's what I believe."

"You're so good. So true. So kind. So generous. So brave. So modest. Haven't you had enough of that cigarette?"

"Good heavens, no," I almost shouted. "We've got to make things last these days."

"You see, I never think of anything. You'll have to punish me, dear. Take me in your arms and just squeeze the life out of me."

The ash on my cigarette was burning down as though somebody were chasing it. I took another one from my pocket.

"Chain smoking!" she cried. "Oh, my poor darling. What they must have done to your nerves over there. I'll make you well again. First I'll put a stop to this chain smoking."

She took the fresh cigarette and the butt out of my hands and threw them in the water. Then she leaned forward expectantly so that I could put my arm behind her.

A sudden burst of courage possessed me. "Estherlee," I said, "there's something I must tell you."

"All right, dear. But hurry. I'm cold." She nuzzled against me, laid her cheek on mine. Her toes curled.

"Nothing," I said.

I slipped my arm behind her while the beast in me snuffed out my conscience with a huge, hairy paw.

CHAPTER XV

THE LADIES of the Hearth and Hauteur Sodality looked at me placidly over the ramparts of their bosoms as I stepped to the rostrum of their meeting room in the Fjord Room of the Scandia Hotel. Mrs. La Hoont, who was easily in the dreadnought class, had just introduced me. "Girls," she had said, "I have a treat for you today. As you know, Mrs. Malheur was going to review *Rebecca* today for her report on Worth-while Classics. We thank her for graciously giving up her time to our special guest." Mrs. Malheur had stood and bowed to the extent of whalebone's flexibility in acknowledgement of the applause. "Our guest today is, as His Honor La Hoont calls him, a true American," Mrs. La Hoont had continued. "You have all read the stirring newspaper account of how his heroism saved an American army in North Africa from destruction by the fascists. The bastards. It is with a deep sense of honor and gratitude that I introduce to you Sergeant Daniel Miller of Minneapolis and the United States Army."

"Ladies," I said with unusual presence of mind for me, "my

little part in the war has already been publicized—you might say overly publicized. Heh, heh. There is nothing more I can tell you. Therefore I propose a reversal in the usual order of these things. Heh, heh. Why don't I stand here and listen while you ladies tell me about *your* part in the war?"

"How utterly charming," said Mrs. La Hoont.

"Utterly," agreed the Hearth and Hauteur.

"Perhaps I'd better start by going back a way," said Mrs. La Hoont. "On the afternoon of December 7, 1941, the Hearth and Hauteur was holding a smörgåsbord meeting to discuss plans for his honor La Hoont's Christmas party for underprivileged Republican children. During the meeting we sent out for some bicarbonate for poor Mrs. Swedenborg, who has a tendency to bloat after eating."

Mrs. Swedenborg interrupted. "Them oysters was spoilt," she belched.

"Yes. Anyway, the bellboy came in with the bicarbonate a few minutes after two. 'The bastards bombed Pearl Harbor,' he said. Well! We were speechless, but only for a few moments. We soon regained our senses. 'This is it,' I said.

" 'Yes,' the girls agreed, 'this is it.'

"Having recognized the danger, we acted with lightning speed. Instantly the Hearth and Hauteur went all out. Several committees were formed on the spot. Mrs. Wripley was put in charge of a committee to study military organization."

Mrs. Wripley stood up. "All army officers are called 'sir' by enlisted men. In the Navy they are called 'matey.' It is considered good form to salute officers upon sight. The salute is executed by bringing the hand to the forehead—thus. In the event that a man is carrying a gun when the officer comes into view, he fires the gun—into the air, of course.

"In the Army strict conformity is demanded in both officers' and enlisted men's dress. Enlisted men may wear only olive-drab blouses and trousers. Officers may wear only olive-drab or dark green blouses, and their trousers are limited to olive drab, dark green, light green, forest green, bottle green, aquamarine, flesh pink, salmon, mauve, fuchsia, tan, russet, or off brown. In the Navy enlisted men wear pocketless leotards of navy blue or white. Naval officers design their own uniforms.

"The Army is divided into divisions, which in turn are divided into regiments, the regiments into companies, and the companies into platoons (pontoons in the engineers' corps). This is slightly varied in the Air Force, where the men are divided into fighters and bombers.

"His Honor President Roosevelt is commander in chief of the Army and Navy."

"Thank you, Mrs. Wripley," said Mrs. La Hoont.

"There's some more, but I forget," said Mrs. Wripley.

"We also," continued His Honor Mayor La Hoont's wife, "named an Alert Committee under the leadership of Mrs. Pinkeye."

Mrs. Pinkeye rose. "In the event that Minneapolis is invaded while the Hearth and Hauteur is holding a meeting, my committee has formed a complete plan." She pointed to a matron who had been leaning precariously out the window all through the meeting. "Mrs. Hambrick over there is our sentry. At the sight of enemy troops she will say, 'Birnam Wood approaches.'"

"Or cheese it, the copse," laughed lighthearted Mrs. Hambrick.

"That is our signal," Mrs. Pinkeye said. "The older women will proceed in an orderly fashion to the basement of the hotel and lock themselves in the meat cooler. The rest of us will put on chambermaids' costumes and go about the hotel dusting and affecting French accents.

"We thought at first that it would be braver to face the bastards just as we were. But later we realized that we could better serve by going into hiding and carrying on our work from underground."

"Thank you, Mrs. Pinkeye," said Mrs. La Hoont. "We also organized a Wartime Substitutes Committee with Mrs. Crutfellow as chairwoman."

Mrs. Crutfellow, a painted crone, reported. "My committee's

work was chiefly to study the relative merits of stick and liquid limb make-up. We performed an experiment. Being a good deal younger than most of these ladies, I volunteered myself as, you might say, the guinea pig.

"On one of my limbs I put stick make-up and on the other liquid make-up. For two weeks there was no difference, but in the third week one make-up flaked away while the other was as good as new. Unfortunately, by that time I had forgotten on which limb I put which make-up."

"Thank you, Mrs. Crutfellow. And we also——"

"I remember some more," interrupted Mrs. Wripley, the authority on military organization. "The artillery concerns itself largely with guns. Some of these guns are mounted on mechanized carriages while others are mounted on horses. The guns range in size from small machine guns to giant howitzers, which fire trajectories. There is also anti-aircraft artillery or flak-flak."

"Thank you, Mrs. Wripley," said Mrs. La Hoont. "A committee to study wartime language usage was set up with Mrs. Plantaganet as chairwoman."

"Wah," said Mrs. Plantaganet in cultured accents, "has wrought vahst changes in the language. It is now propah—in fact *à la mode*—to speak of the enemy as 'bahstards.' 'Ahss,' too, is allowed in connection with an infantry retreat. One may say, 'The infantry is hauling ahss.' Howevah, this term is used only in speaking of *our* infantry. When the enemy, or bahstard, infantry haul *their* ahss, we do not speak of it in that mannah.

"What this new freedom of language will lead to one can only conjecture. My committee, howevah, is quietly preparing for the day when all barriahs are let down and the four-lettah functional words become propah usage. We are meeting for lunch once a week in a little tearoom and speaking to each othah in these terms. That is, we *were* meeting up to lahst week, when the tearoom proprietress had us arrested."

"Thank you, Mrs. Plantaganet. And there are many more committees—too numerous to mention now," said Mrs. La Hoont, to the ill-disguised dismay of the chairwomen of the slighted committees. "They are all, each and every one, doing work equally as important as those you have heard about. And, Sergeant Miller, all of these committees were formed the day of Pearl Harbor. The bastards might have caught the Hearth and Hauteur by surprise, but we were quick to rally.

"The work goes on today. We will not rest until the bastards are beaten."

"That's keen, Mrs. La Hoont," I said.

"I'll be frank with you," said Mrs. La Hoont, being frank with me. "The Hearth and Hauteur could carry on an ordinary type war program—rolling bandages, knitting and sewing, operating canteens, working in blood banks, baking cookies—that type thing. In its way that type work has a certain value. It certainly reflects credit on the type women who are doing it. But we ladies have enjoyed certain advantages. We are capable of a higher type war program. Really, Sergeant Miller, if we didn't carry on this type war program, we would not be giving of ourselves to the fullest. And in this total war, as His Honor La Hoont calls it, one must give to one's fullest. Don't you agree?"

"Clearly," said I. "Well, thank you, ladies. I've learned a great deal."

"Thank *you*, Sergeant Miller," said Mrs. La Hoont, "for a most inspirational talk."

"Don't mention it," I said.

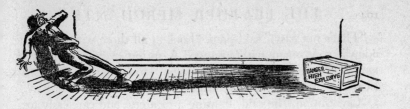

CHAPTER XVI

At eight o'clock that night Sam Wye called for me in a Stutz Bearcat with which his father had won the presidency of Sigma Chi in 1920. "Put on your linen duster and let's get going," he called.

I got in gingerly. "What's that in the back seat?" I asked, pointing at a black wooden box.

"Dynamite."

"Please, Sam, let's take my car. It's got brakes, springs, upholstery. Rides like a little dream. You don't even know you're moving."

"You ought to work for Gelt and Gelt," said Sam as he pulled out from the curb with a roaring lurch.

With closed eyes I heard a blast that I was sure must be the last trump. "Keep your eyes open, Roberto," said Sam. "That one I just honked at was strictly your type. With slacks yet. She walked like a fat metronome."

I leaped into the back seat and got a death grip on the black box.

"Careful you don't get that stuff too warm holding it," said Sam. "A little overheating and she'll go blooie, just like that."

I leaped back into the front seat. "Sam," I said thickly, "do me a personal favor and drive more carefully. Look at that stuff shaking around back there. NO! Don't look around now. You can take my word for it. Keep your eyes on the road."

"That's not easy," said Sam. "Look at all those women on the sidewalks. Women without men. A spring evening. The goat song of the flesh. Ah, passion, passion. How quickly it can strip away the thin veneer of civilization.

"Civilization," he said, lighting a cigarette and carelessly tossing the match into the back seat, an act that speeded my demise by at least ten years, "what mockery. I am in mind of my uncle Cantripp, probably the most civilized man I ever knew. An archaeologist by profession, he had degrees from a dozen universities. His home was filled with books, paintings, symphonic records. He spoke only in complete sentences, usually containing dependent clauses. Even in the bathtub he sang nothing more frivolous than a Gregorian chant. A civilized man.

"Well, sir, one summer he went with an archaeological expedition into the jungles of Guatemala. Somehow he became separated from his party, and he wandered through the jungle until he was captured by a tribe of savages. Being the first white man they had ever seen, he was an object of much curiosity to the tribe—particularly to their princess, a café-au-lait wench named Mendel-Fendel. She took Uncle Cantripp to her scalp-festooned personal lodge, and there she kept him very well.

"For years nobody back home heard of him. At length an intrepid New York reporter named Stanley went into the jungle to look for him. After many months of searching, Stanley was rewarded. It took all of his persuasive wiles, however, to get Uncle Cantripp to leave his Mendel-Fendel and go home.

"Uncle Cantripp came home, but he didn't stay long. His aging wife, my aunt Iris, was sufficiently ardent but not spry enough to please him after Mendel-Fendel. Within a year he was back in Guatemala.

"He went to Mendel-Fendel's lodge, persuaded Stanley that *he* ought to go home, and lived happily ever after."

We were near the edge of the city now, and I sighed with relief that there were no more women on the sidewalks to distract Sam. I settled back with a slight degree of comfort as we rolled onto the broad, smooth highway leading out of town. But suddenly Sam swung off the highway upon a rutted dirt side road. "Sam!" I screamed. "For God's sake, why did you leave the highway?"

"We'll save twenty minutes on this cutoff," he explained.

The black box was bounding crazily on the back seat. "Sam! Sam!"

"Peace, Roberto," he said calmly. "There's only three miles of this."

"Only three miles!"

"All right, if you're nervous I'll step on the gas. It won't take so long then."

The road was like a cardiograph of a Cheyne-Stokes respiration. At every bump the box leaped to the ceiling of the car, hit with a thud, and plummeted back to the seat. Occasionally it bounced from the ceiling to the floor and back to the seat again with a *plop, ploop, dong, ploop* effect, a sort of grisly conga. I prayed rapidly to the Christian, Jewish, and Mohammedan gods and then, to be on the safe side, to Buddha, Jupiter, and Vishnu. I had a go at Zoroaster, Isis, Osiris, and Re. I was on Dundik, an obscure Druid deity, when we got back on the pavement.

"My God," said Sam, "you're tattletale gray. Look at you. You're ghastly. Man, you need a drink."

I croaked assent.

"Well, well," said Sam, "there's a tavern right up the road. Fancy that. Why, it looks like the Sty. You remember the Sty."

"Drive on!" I shrieked. "I don't want to go to the Sty."

"There's not another joint for miles, and you need something right now."

"No. I'm all right now."

"O.K., if you say so, friend. But I do think we ought to stop and let the dynamite rest for a while. Sometimes that stuff gets shaken up and nothing happens, but a few minutes later— BAM! But if you don't want to stop here——"

"Stop."

He pulled into the parking lot in front of the Sty. "A couple of Sty Stingers and you'll be right back in the pink," he said jovially.

"Look, we're just going to the bar. We're not going in and sit down. And we're going to leave in five minutes."

"Sure, sure."

I pulled my flight cap low over my face, which is a good trick, and we went inside to the bar. "Two Sty Stingers," said Sam. The barkeep served us. I drained mine at a gulp and started away. "You're being rather rude, you know," said Sam. "I've scarcely tasted mine."

"I'll wait for you in the car."

"I wouldn't," he warned. "Better give that dynamite a few more minutes to cool off. That stuff's treacherous. I saw a fellow pick up a stick of it once, and the next minute he was standing there without——"

"Another one of these," I said to the bartender without waiting for Sam to finish.

"Well, for crying out loud!" boomed a voice behind us that could belong only to P.B. Gelt. "It's Daniel Miller and Montag Fortz. Isn't it, Al?"

"Yes," said Al.

"You rascal," said P.B., whirling me around and pumping my hand. "The other night you told us your name was Robert Jordan."

"Modest," explained Sam.

"You boys are coming inside and sit at our table," roared P.B. "No hero is going to pay for no drink while I'm around, by God. You neither, Fortz. It still bothers me about your mother."

"She was only in the way," said Sam.

"Thank you kindly," I said, "but we have to be going."

"You should let that stuff sit for at least half an hour," Sam hissed to me. "Why, sure, Mr. Gelt. Lead the way."

I was not surprised to see a pair of twin girls sitting at the Gelts' table when we got there. "Daniel Miller and Montag Fortz," said P.B., "I want you to meet a damn fine pair of girls.

The Replevin twins, Ruth and Rachel. Only twins ever born on a Minneapolis streetcar."

The Replevins sat there with all the sparkle of dictionary illustrations. "How do you do?" they droned. "We read all about you in the paper, Sergeant Miller. We think you're wonderful. Can we each take one of you home? We just bought two used cars from the Gelt brothers."

"Now, now, girls," chided P.B. "Don't you know you're supposed to go home with the man you come with?"

"We're not very bright," admitted the Replevins.

"Yes," said Al.

P.B. ordered a round of Sty Stingers. "I was thinking of you this afternoon, Miller," he said. "I happened to make a lucky buy today and I got hold of a car that's just right for a hero. It's a '34 Chrysler with no top, so you can drive around and wave to admiring crowds. Good as new, too. Fellow that owned it got killed two days after he bought it in an argument with a Baptist fanatic over total immersion. I'll sacrifice it to you for $950, cash or terms."

"I'll think it over," I told him.

The waiter brought the drinks. I finished mine quickly. "We don't like to drink," the Replevins confessed. "Every time we drink we get helpless and men take advantage of us, and we can't help it because we're helpless."

I stood up. "Thanks for the drinks, P.B. We hate to run, but we've really got to."

"Where?" came a feminine shriek from across the room.

"There!" answered another. "Follow me."

Blanche came loping off the dance floor with Madge close behind her. A pair of balding, disappointed men who had been planning big things for later that evening pursued them both. The men gave up the chase midway in answer to an invitation from a pair of hot-eyed lady welders.

"I told you it was them," said Blanche triumphantly as they skidded into our table. "Hello, dears."

"Why, Blanche and Madge," said Sam with real pleasure. "How nice to see you again. Won't you sit down?"

"Yes," said I. "Make yourselves comfortable. We have to be running along now. P.B. will buy you a drink in memory of Montag's mother. Won't you, P.B.?"

"It's the least I can do," he said.

"Come along, Montag."

"I don't think it's time yet," he said smilingly. "We'd better sit down for a few more minutes. Remember? Bang-bang. Gooey-gooey youey-youey."

I sat down. "Montag," I said, "you should go far in the engineers. You engineered me in here nicely tonight."

"Why, Dan!" he said, hurt.

"Well, let's all have a drink," proposed P.B. He ordered eight Sty Stingers. "Mrs. Gooberman and Mrs. Spetalnik, I want you to meet Ruth and Rachel Replevin."

"How do you do?" said the twins. "We dyed our hair once. It came out even worse than yours."

"They're not very bright," said Sam quickly. "Tell me, girls, what have you been doing since we saw you last?"

"Dearie," said Madge, "a terrible thing happened to me. Last night I am entertaining a tool and die maker in my flat when in walks Rex—that's Mr. Spetalnik. 'Who is this man?' he says.

"'Who are you?' asks the tool and die maker.

"'I'm her husband,' says Rex, although we been divorced now six months.

"'A con game,' says the tool and die maker. 'I been tricked.'

"'Well, of all the nerve,' says I. 'Accusing me of running a con game. I'll have you know that this is a high-class establishment. Please to take your things and go.'

"Well, I bum-rushed him the hell out of there, and I turns on Rex and says, 'Now will you please explain what is the grand idea you busting into my place with manure on your feet and driving off my friends?'"

The waiter interrupted with our drinks. "Hang on to your

cash-register checks, folks," he said. "They got your Spin-O numbers on 'em."

"It's about time we were going, isn't it, Montag?" I said.

"Please," he protested. "The lady is right in the middle of a story."

"You bastard," I muttered into my drink. "You're fixing to railroad me again tonight."

"How come you told us your name was Jordan last time?" asked Blanche.

"Modest," Sam explained.

"We're getting more and more helpless," announced the Replevins.

" 'Now, don't get sore,' Rex says," continued Madge. " 'I just came up here to ask you a question.'

" 'Well, hurry up and ask it and get the hell off the rug,' I told him. 'Last time I sent that rug to the cleaners' they refused it.'

" 'I want to ask you about that cod-liver oil I been taking,' he says. 'Am I supposed to take a teaspoon of cod-liver oil with a glass of water or a glass of cod-liver oil with a teaspoon of water?'

" 'A teaspoon of cod-liver oil with a glass of water, you jerk,' I says.

" 'My God,' he says, 'no wonder I been scared to go out of the house on Fridays.' "

I finished my Sty Stinger. "Montag, it's time."

"Everybody have your cash-register checks ready," called the m.c. "It's time to play Spin-O. Miss Fligg, will you please come up and spin the magic wheel?"

Miss Fligg came up to the wheel, dipped her leg through the slit in her gown in a low curtsy, and spun the wheel around. "Number 162," she announced. "Will the lucky winner step forward?"

"That's you," Blanche screeched, pulling me to my feet. "Get up there."

I threw my ticket under the table rapidly. "No, you're wrong," I said desperately.

Sam swooped under the table and retrieved my ticket. "Number 162," he said. "That's you, Dan." He pushed me forward.

"I'll get you for this," I snarled.

"Well," crowed Miss Fligg, "well, well, well. It's Daniel Miller, folks. The hero."

Led by Sam, the audience applauded wildly.

"Well, dearie," said Miss Fligg, "I got a real nice prize for you. Here, take a look at it." She handed me a black wooden box. I jumped back six or eight feet. "It won't hurt you," she laughed. "I'll open it." To my immeasurable relief it contained a bottle of scotch packed in straw. "Real stuff," Miss Fligg assured me. "Not what I sell here. But before I give it to you I think you ought to say a few words to the folks."

"It's a pleasure," I said. With the determination of a long-suffering man in overdue revolt and the confidence born of four Sty Stingers I stepped firmly to the microphone. "Ladies and gentlemen, it would be a shocking thing for me to stand here and pretend to be a hero." I smiled as I saw Sam go white. "What I have done," I continued, "is no more than what any soldier would have done in the line of duty. I am no hero.

"But there is a hero, a real hero, with us tonight. He's sitting over there at the table I just left. His name is Sam Wye. S-A-M W-Y-E. He is very modest and calls himself Montag Fortz. But his name is Sam Wye. S-A-M W-Y-E. Remember it."

"He's drunk," yelled Sam.

"See how modest he is," I said. "He doesn't want me to tell what he has done. But such deeds as he has performed must be told. The people have a right to know. On Guadalcanal Sam Wye—S-A-M W-Y-E—alone and unarmed, captured one hundred and twenty Japs. He made a sarong out of a shelter half, put a couple of coconuts in it, fixed his hair in an upsweep, and, thus disguised as a Geisha girl, enticed one hundred and twenty Japs into the American camp, where they were taken alive."

The patrons stamped and whistled, and Madge rained wet kisses on Sam.

"There's more," I said. "He's not only a hero, he's a secret weapon. He has destroyed more than fifty U-boats by diving under water and punching holes in their sides with a dirk."

Now the customers began showering coins and a little folding money on him. "He's out of his head," cried Sam. "His nerves are gone."

"Ah, modest Sam Wye—S-A-M W-Y-E," I said lovingly. "And now let me tell you his crowning feat, probably the most daring exploit of a United States soldier in all history. He parachuted into the imperial palace in Tokyo, kidnaped Hirohito, rowed him across the Pacific in a rubber boat to San Francisco, where he is now a prisoner in the Mark Hopkins Hotel!"

Now there were no coins—just folding money.

"Thank you, ladies and gentlemen. Now I will take my prize and go sit at the feet of my hero, Sam Wye—S-A-M W-Y-E."

"You bastard," he cursed after I had fought my way through the crowd around our table. "You bastard."

"Do you think it's time to go now?" I asked in high good humor.

He rose quickly and we bucked our way out. "Hey," called P.B. Gelt, "if you're not Fortz, then I didn't kill your mother, did I, Al?"

"No," said Al.

I put my wooden box containing the scotch in the back seat next to the dynamite, and Sam drove the Stutz Bearcat away in silence. "You're not mad, are you, Sammy?" I asked, feeling very good.

He didn't answer for a few minutes. "No, I'm not mad," he said finally. "Just a little hurt, that's all."

I glowed happily.

"Well, what's done is done," he philosophized. "We've got work to do now. There's an old bridge a few miles west of the highway. It's on an old abandoned farm. We'll go blow that up. I think I can find it."

"O.K., Sammy," I said genially.

He swung abruptly off the highway. The cutoff he had taken before we stopped at the Sty was an air cushion compared to what we were driving over now. There was no road. We were going forty miles an hour over open fields, newly furrowed before the spring planting. The two boxes in the back seat leaped and bounded and clashed together like lethal castanets. They caromed off the sides of the car, met in the middle of the seat, recoiled, and were slammed to the floor only to bounce back to the seat and then the sides and the ceiling and the seat and floor once more.

"Sam!" I hollered in mortal terror. "Sam!"

We plunged in and out of a mudhole, and I heard the wood crack in the two boxes. "Sam! What are you doing?"

"What's the difference?" he said. "Nothing matters any more."

"What are you—Sam!—talking about? Nothing matters any more. Do you think I got you in—Sam!—trouble? Look what you did to me. At least there were no news—Sam!—papermen around when I put the blocks to you. You're the guy that told me not to —Sam!—worry, and now you're acting like this."

"I'm not worried," he said, crashing through a picket fence ("Sam!"). "I'm just hurt and disappointed that you should do such a thing to me."

There was a stream straight ahead. He couldn't possibly be thinking of—— He pressed harder on the accelerator. "SAM! SAM! Stop the car! Now! This minute! Stop the car!"

He screeched to a stop on the brink of the stream. I reached into the back seat, opened the box that contained the scotch, and took a long, deep pull. Then I dropped the bottle and leaped out of the car and ran to a haystack three hundred yards away and covered myself.

Sam came over shortly with the bottle. "Don't you want to get there? It's only a couple of miles more."

I trembled negatively.

"How am I going to teach you demolition if you won't let me?"

"Please," I croaked. "Let's not even talk about it. Let's wait a little while for the dynamite to cool off and then you take me home."

"If you say so." He gave me the bottle, and I drank eagerly.

"Yes, Dan," he said, "that was a shoddy thing you did to me tonight."

"Oh, come off that. Look what you did to me."

"I'll admit it. But I was trying to make amends. I was devoting my last night before I went overseas to teaching you demolition. I was actually risking my life for you. It's the easiest thing in the world to get killed playing around with dynamite."

I hit the bottle again, hard.

"Well, let's forget about it," he said. "It's good to find out who your friends are."

We sat silently. Occasionally I would begin to shake, and I would pour another slug of scotch in me. More than half the bottle went to quiet my tremors.

At the end of a half hour Sam said it was safe, and we went back to the car. "Please drive slowly," I begged.

He nodded. He drove carefully across the field back to the highway. On the highway he drove well under thirty. I leaned back on the seat. The night air, the scotch, and the Sty Stingers were affecting me strangely. I put the bottle of scotch back in the box in the back seat. We drove some more, and a great sense of sadness came over me. By the time we were back in the city I was sniffling.

"That's all right, Danny," said Sam. "It doesn't matter about me."

I'm not sure that that was what I was crying about, but it seemed logical at the time. "Sam," I said, "I did a shoddy thing to you tonight."

"That's all right," said Sam.

"Tomorrow you're going overseas, and you spend your last night at home risking your life teaching me demolition, and I do a shoddy thing like that to you."

"It's O.K., Dan. Forget it."

"It's shoddy. That's what it is, shoddy."

I sat abjectly until we were in front of my house. "Sam, I want you to know that no matter how shoddily I acted tonight, I'm grateful to you. And if you'll accept my good wishes, I want to wish you the best of luck when you go across. And I hope we will soon be together again, on which occasion I will do my best to try to repay you for what you have done."

"Thank you," he said simply.

"Now you must go get some sleep. It's shoddy of me to keep you up."

I offered him my hand and he shook it warmly. "Good-by, Sam," I said thickly. "We've been good friends, haven't we?"

"Yes, Roberto. Don't forget your scotch."

I reached back and picked up the box. "The other one," he said gently.

"I could have sworn it was this one."

"No, Dan, the other one."

"Thank you, Sam. You're so good to me, and I'm so shoddy."

I took the box and staggered to the door of my house, waving at Sam long after he had gone. I found my way upstairs to my room, threw the box on the bed, and switched on the light. Then I saw that I had taken the dynamite box.

I leaped frantically under the bureau, where I lay shuddering. When nothing happened for several minutes, I stuck my head out cautiously. The box lay quietly on my bed. The lid had come off. I crawled closer.

It was empty.

CHAPTER XVII

AT TEN THE NEXT MORNING O. Merriam Phyfe deposited me in a bunting-draped recruiting booth on a busy downtown corner. "ENLIST WITH SERGEANT DANIEL (DANNY BOY) MILLER, OUR OWN HERO" said a banner tacked across the front of the booth. "Here's a pile of literature, Danny Boy," said Phyfe, "and there's a stack of enlistment blanks. You'll stay here until noon. Then you'll go to the studio for your radio interview with Colonel Swatch. After that you'll pitch the first ball at the Minneapolis baseball opener. Is that all clear?"

"Yes."

"Good. Remember, the eyes of Minneapolis and His Honor Mayor La Hoont are upon you. Carry on, Danny Boy."

"Good-by, Phyfey Boy."

I sat unhappily waiting for business. A few 4-Fs limped smugly by and some 3-As nervously crossed to the other side of the street.

At length some women stopped. One made me promise to see what I could do about getting her son off K.P.; one wanted information on how to attach her common-law husband's pay; one went over me with a tapeline to get my measurements for a sweater for her son, who she reckoned was about my size; one misinformed trollop wanted to know how to get installed in an army prophylactic station; one tearfully brought me a Pomeranian for the Wags; one told me to tell Corporal Ed Gilroy, if I ran into him, that everything was all right—that stuff he sent her did the trick; one shook a finger at me and demanded to know why I got a furlough while her son had to stay in New Caledonia; one with seven small children said she'd be beholden to the government if her husband was drafted, and five tried to pick me up.

My time was almost up when a man finally stopped, if such he could be called. His face was stippled with pimples, and his voice was right off the Henry Aldrich program. "Danny Boy," he said, "I can't make up my mind. What I want to do is kill a lot of them bastards. Eh-eh-eh-eh-eh-eh-eh-eh." He made like a machine gun. He bayoneted a few of the corpses and whirled and picked off a sniper on top of the bank building across the street. "Got him," he said.

"There's one in Walgreen's doorway," I warned.

He turned and fired twice. "There was two," he explained. "Boy, I could kill them bastards all day. Now, look. I'll be eighteen in a few months, and——"

"How many months?" I asked.

"Sixteen. And I'm trying to figure out what outfit I can join where I can kill the most of them bastards. First I thought I'd be a bombardier. They do a hell of a lot of killing. Then I thought, so I'm a bombardier, I'm ten thousand feet in the air, I drop my bombs, and five seconds later I'm gone. How do I know I killed anybody? No, bombardier is out.

"It's the same with artillery. You're too far away to see how many you kill. Machine guns is pretty good, but they don't get enough to suit me. I want to kill a *lot* of them bastards. Rifle, of course, is out of the question. I can't make up my mind.

"Now, tell me. Is there some kind of mysterious death ray I can learn to operate?"

"Not that I know of," I answered.

"I can't make up my mind," he said, and walked off leaving the unburied dead behind him.

The receptionist was holding Colonel Swatch at bay with a letter opener when I entered the radio studio. "Thank God you're here," she said devoutly.

"Ah, Sergeant Miller," said Swatch. "You're just in time. We're on the air in a few minutes. Come into Studio A."

I followed him into Studio A. We sat down on opposite sides of a table that had a small microphone on top of it. "Just a moment, Sergeant," said the colonel. He walked over and goosed the lady organist.

"God damn it!" she cried. "Do you think it's easy to play this thing standing up?"

"Now, Sergeant," he said, coming back satisfied, "this is going to be an informal interview. Just forget that I'm an officer. We won't need a script. I'll ask you questions, and you just answer them simply. There's the red light. We're on in a few seconds."

The engineer signaled to the organist, who bent over and played the theme. Then the announcer told the world that for this day it would be deprived of Colonel Swatch's usual analysis of the war, but that he would instead interview Minneapolis' newest hero, the nonpareil Sergeant Daniel (Hard Rock) Miller.

"Well, Hard Rock," said the colonel, "how does it feel to be home?"

"Great," I answered.

"Yes, it's always great to get home from the wars. I recollect a furlough I had from the Spanish-American War. It was a sick leave; I had received a ball in my temple in the charge up San Juan Hill. I was put in a Minneapolis hospital in the care of a 140-pound nurse. Woman was demented. She thought purgatives were the universal specific. I finally demanded to be sent back to combat."

"You still had the ball in your temple?"

"Yes, I had that until 1911, when it popped out during a rough train ride near Pierre, South Dakota. It seems that the Indian section hands who laid the tracks in that stretch didn't understand English and confused their orders. They put the ties on *top* of the rails. Damn redskins."

"That was a shoddy thing they did to Custer," I said.

"Hard Rock, that is the blackest page in American history," said the colonel. "George was a great-minded man. Always had his wits about him. I recall one time George and I were in Vera Cruz on an important government mission. In the evenings, for a little relaxation, you understand, we trifled with a pair of acquiescent young women who lived on the water front. One night their husbands, who ordinarily worked on the swing shift at a bean gleanery, returned unexpectedly. George and I fled with the heavily armed Mexicans in close pursuit. We finally eluded them, jumped into a fishing sloop, and sailed out into the tuna-fishing waters off the coast. For days we stayed hidden in the bottom of our boat while the vengeful husbands scoured the bay. At last one day they pulled up beside our tuna boat. 'Who's in there?' they demanded. I thought we were done for. But not George. 'Nobody here but us chickens of the sea,' he answered."

"A great-minded man," I admitted.

"Great-stomached, too. I recollect one time George had got a gallon of bourbon that he was saving for his birthday. The night before his birthday, for a prank, I poured the bourbon out of the jug and filled it with the fluid that drains off a keg of nails. Came his birthday, George drank that whole jug without even making a face. It didn't affect him a bit, either, except for the rest of his life whenever he saw a hammer he'd scream and cover his head."

"A great-stomached man," I concurred.

"Great hearted, too. I remember one night we were out driving in a new surrey that George had just bought from P.B. Gelt, the elder, when George's horse saw a mare in a yard across the street. He whirled around, leaped a picket fence, and smashed that surrey to kindling.

" 'George,' I said to him, 'you ought to have that horse gelded.'

" 'For shame, Cosmo,' he answered. 'How would you like someone to do that to you?' "

"There will now be a brief interlude of organ music," interrupted the announcer hastily.

"Come on into the locker room," said John Smith, who was waiting for me at the ball park. "I want you to meet some of the athletes."

I followed him into the locker room, where the players were relaxing before the opening game. "This is our starting pitcher, Lefty Gemutlich," said Smith, introducing me to a venerable gentleman who was sitting in a rocker while his grandson read him the *Sporting News*. "Lefty was with the Cubs for many years."

"I'd still be with 'em," quavered Lefty, "only I thrun my arm out in '28."

"And this is Lefty Febrish, our catcher. This is his first year with the club."

"Hi, Danny Boy," said Lefty Febrish. "I still can't make up my mind." He was the kid who had stopped at the recruiting booth in the morning.

"And here's a shortstop I'm sure you know—Lefty Mashou-lam."

Of course I knew him. Who hasn't heard of Wagner to Cobb to Mashoulam?

"I'm gonna have a comeback this year," said Lefty Gemutlich, the pitcher. "I got a new floater pitch. I don't have to thrun so hard."

"This is one of the most unusual athletes in baseball," said John Smith. "In spite of losing his left arm up to the shoulder in a railroad accident, he is one of the finest third basemen in the business. I want you to meet No Lefty Monahue."

"I been pitchin' with my head since I thrun my arm out," said Lefty Gemutlich.

"And here is Lefty Paternoster, the only unfrocked priest in baseball."

"Pax," said Lefty Paternoster.

"This is Lefty Frotheringham, the noted British athlete."

"I say," said Lefty Frotheringham, "this baseball *is* like cricket, isn't it?"

"And here is Lefty Goldfarb, our right fielder."

"Right fielder, shmight fielder," shrugged Lefty Goldfarb. "One day I am delivering the team's uniforms from mine shop, and the next minute I am a right fielder, right shmielder."

"If they change the rules like they was talkin' about, so you can thrun underhand," said Lefty Gemutlich, "I will be soon back in the majors. I thrun underhand good."

"Here is our center fielder, Lefty Chisholm, who should turn into a great attraction," said John Smith, introducing me to a mounted gentleman.

"Hiya, podner," said Lefty Chisholm. "They're lettin' me play on my hoss. Been ridin' sincet I was two. Never did learn to walk."

"I thrun a ball to a man once from the top of the Washington Monument," said Lefty Gemutlich. "Drove him two feet into the pavement."

The trainer came in with a pot of beef tea and a flagon of adrenalin. "Time for your pre-game booster, boys," he said.

In a little while they were strong enough to go out on the diamond. I went out and threw the first ball, a sidearm curve that broke nicely over the outside corner. Then, rejecting a contract, I took a hasty departure.

CHAPTER XVIII

ONE DAY REMAINED before the grand finale, and I intended to spend it wisely. As soon as I was able to move after Mama's breakfast, I hied myself off to the public library, took out three books on demolition for amateurs, and sat down to bone up as much as I could before the next day's ordeal.

It was a cold day. The reading room was filled with unemployables who had left the Missions too late to get seats at District Court. Those with neckties read *Fortune,* those without neckties read newspapers, and those without shirts looked up dirty words in Webster's International.

The character sitting next to me was somewhat difficult to classify. He had a necktie but no shirt, and he was reading an astrology book written in French. Moreover, he wore pince-nez and had a carefully trimmed goatee. He gave me three minutes to get settled before he began the inevitable conversation.

"How do you do, my good?" he said. "Permit me. I am Jean-Pierre d'Estoppel."

"Name of Miller," I said, shaking his unwashed hand.

"Sergeant, no?"

"Yes."

"I can tell by your sleeve. There were many Americains in my village during the Great War. My father was in the French Army. He was shot twice in the *poilu* at Verdun. Killed, of course."

"I'm sorry."

"It is the life," he shrugged. "Who can tell what will happen?" He held up the astrology book. "I now study this astrology. Perhaps here is the answer. Ah, my young, if one could only know what is in the future. If one could only know. Do you think I would be here today in these rags if I could have know, eh? Let me tell you."

What the hell, I said to myself as I closed my demolition book and got comfortable.

"If I could have know, I would never have got on the packet *Duncan Leprechaun II* and sailed away from my native Provence that day in 1921. My maman done told don't go, but I said, 'Don't you worry, Maman. I will be back a rich man, and meanwhile you will soon get the pension for poor dead Papan.' If I could have know!

"But Maman's pleas were soon forgotten. I became absorbed in the gay whirl of steerage life aboard the *Duncan Leprechaun II,* and soon I was making hot Gallic overtures to a young Americain widow who had lately been freed for shooting her husband because he kept saying to her, 'Why can't you be like Mabel Normand?' Yes, my little, it was a bon voyage and it seemed to foretell all good things. How droll!

"For when I arrived in New York I learned quickly that the streets were not paved with gold. For months I trudged the unfriendly streets looking for work while my meager savings dwindled and finally disappeared. I would certainly have starved had I not finally secured a job as a food taster for an apprehensive Tammany alderman.

"Then one morning I happened to look at a newspaper that had been my blanket the night before as I slept on a park bench. It was a Minneapolis newspaper, and in it I found an advertisement for a teacher of French at the Harold Stassen High School.

The heart within me leaped. I sent off an application by first post and was shortly answered with an acceptance and a railroad ticket to Minneapolis.

"How I blessed my good fortune then! Ha! What a mockery. If I could have know, I would have torn that ticket to bits. Instead I boarded the first train to Minneapolis. In the smoking car I became involved in a conversation with a man who, if I could have know, I would have avoided as the pox. We talked casually of this and that, and then I introduced myself.

" 'How do you do?' he said. 'My name is Duncan Leprechaun.'

" 'But what a coincidence!' I cried. 'The ship that brought me to this country was also called *Duncan Leprechaun.*'

" 'Well, well, well,' he said.

"We talked on. Because of the simple wonder of a duplication in names I felt closer to this stranger than to anyone since I had come to this unfriendly land. Without meaning to I was soon pouring out my whole story to Duncan Leprechaun. He listened with more attentiveness than is ordinary in a chance acquaintance, but that I did not notice. His close questions I answered with friendly alacrity. If I could have know!

"Then he invited me to the club car, where over a bottle of Florida water he told me a most strange tale. He told me that as a boy he had attended Harold Stassen High School and in the very French classroom where I was to teach he had met and loved a girl named Mary Ellen Nye. She, sadly, had perished in the early blight of '07, brought on, some say, by Halley's comet. Now he asked this of me: would I give him a duplicate key to my classroom so that he could come in the evenings and sit alone and dream sadly poignant dreams of his departed Mary Ellen?

"My young, I am a Frenchman. I promised him the key. If I could have know!

"Now, let me get a little ahead of my story, so that you can better understand what transpired. These things I tell you now I did not learn until much later. Duncan Leprechaun, if I could have know, was a most unscrupulous rogue. Instead of sitting at night in my classroom pining for Mary Ellen, if there ever was such a person, he began to operate a gambling hell. Through means best know to men of his stripe, he let it be known that gambling of all varieties could be had nightly in the French classroom of the Harold Stassen High School. Before long he had an enormous clientele, and the wages of his base profession mounted prodigiously.

"I knew nought of this. Each night I went home to my humble flat, cooked an anchorite's meal on a primus stove whose mechanism I never fully understood, and went to sleep on my pallet. I never went to my classroom at night because I did not want to intrude on Duncan Leprechaun's tender reverie. Ha! I never should have learned of his deception had it not been for Tekla Torkelquist.

"Again I must get ahead of my story. Tekla Torkelquist was a young but lavishly developed woman who was a student in my French class. She was an execrable student because her mind was always on a loose-moraled drayman named Marvin Glander, with whom she was carrying on a sordid affair. One winter night when it was too cold out of doors for that which was on their minds Tekla suggested to Marvin that they utilize her French classroom. He made no objections. They entered the high school, paused in the corridor for some erotic byplay, and then ran hotly into the French classroom. They found Duncan Leprechaun's activities in full session. Alarmed by their sudden intrusion, he rushed over to them, but they assured him that his secret was safe with them and said, as a matter of fact, that they would like to join the play. Nothing loath, Leprechaun seated them at a gaming table. From that night on they were steady patrons.

"But what has this to do with my discovery of Duncan Leprechaun, you are thinking. Listen, my good. Tekla—she did not know it, although it should have been obvious to her that it would one day happen—was with child. As is common with women in such a condition, she felt a strange craving. She wanted to eat chalk—a preference not unknown among pregnant women. Each night while gambling in my classroom she slyly reached out and snatched pieces of chalk from the trays along-side the blackboards and, unobserved, popped them into her mouth.

"That is how I found out. Each morning when I came to class I noticed that there was more and more chalk missing. Finally, in spite of not wishing to disturb Duncan Leprechaun as he mourned the passing of Mary Ellen, I determined to investigate. I concealed myself under a desk one evening after school and waited for the chalk thief to make his appearance. It so happened that I had been kept awake most of the previous night by the wailing of a flatulent infant next door, and I was tired. After an hour's vigil under the desk I dozed off.

"When I awoke I saw all. The room was filled with people recklessly gambling away their substance for the enrichment of Duncan Leprechaun. That brigand strolled about the tables, smilingly taking his percentages from the play. I wanted to cry out in rage, but prudence kept me silent. Choosing a moment when nobody was looking, I crept out of the room.

"I went immediately to a telephone and notified the gen-darmerie. Now, I said to myself, that wretch will pay for his treachery. Now he will get his deserts. If I could have know!

"I reckoned, my young, without the cunning of such as Duncan Leprechaun. Upon apprehension he immediately said that he was but a hireling in his low enterprise, that I, Jean-Pierre d'Estoppel, was the brains of the outfit. What could I, a poor immigrant Frenchman, do against such a devil? No matter how I protested, no matter how often I repeated my story, they would not believe me. 'Damn wops,' said the magistrate. 'I can tell 'em a mile away.'

"And when Tekla Torkelquist, with unspeakable debasement, charged me with the paternity of her child, my doom was sealed. Ten years at hard labor, my little. Ten years.

"And in the village of Provence, where my maman waited for the French civil service to finally begin paying her the pension for my poor dead papan, there occurred the crowning infamy. Maman was about to get the pension when the claims' administrator, a fanatic moralist, learned of my incarceration. 'For mothers of criminals,' he cried, 'the Republic of France has no money.' Instead, then, of living out her life in moderate comfort, Maman was forced to eke out a precarious living laying poultices at the local four-bed hospital until the day of her death.

"If I could have know!"

I patted Jean-Pierre's shoulder. "Now, if you don't mind, I will return to my books," I said.

"By all means," said Jean-Pierre. "May one ask what kind of books they are?"

"Demolition."

"Well, good reading, my young."

I read about three pages when I heard Jean-Pierre mumbling, "Sergeant. Miller. Demolition." Suddenly he slapped the table and cried, "You are Sergeant Miller, the great demolitionist, the hero of Morocco. You are the one who will blow up the bridge at the arms factory tomorrow, yes?"

"Yes."

"Ha, ha!" he roared. "How droll! You, the great demolitionist, are sitting here reading about demolition. As though there were something you didn't know about it. How droll! I must tell the fellows. Say, Gimpy, No-Nose, T.B., Sterno, Dehorn, come over here. I will show you a droll thing."

"Buy bonds!" I called, and was gone.

CHAPTER XIX

THE COLD SNAP precluded canoeing that night, so Estherlee and I spent a quiet evening at home. Before I arrived she had lit the gas log, moved the settee in front of the fire, cooked a cake, and sent her parents to a late movie. Now, in a slinky house coat, she was leaning on my shoulder while I persistently ate cake.

"I'm so thrilled about tomorrow," she said. "Aren't you thrilled?"

"Thrilled isn't precisely the word," I said morosely.

"You know, darling, it's really hard to picture you blowing up a bridge. You're such a fine, sensitive person—so unlike the type person who blows up bridges."

"Yes," I agreed.

"That's what's so wonderful about you, dear. Although you're not a bit warlike, the urgency of the occasion has made you a fierce and terrible fighter. A great man of peace has become a great man of war."

"Let me tell you about soldiers who work in offices, Estherlee."

"Oh, my poor darling! Your plate of cake is empty. I'll get you some more."

Unhappily I watched her undulate into the kitchen after more cake. Unhappily I watched her return. I knew already how the evening would end, how much deeper I would sink into the quicksand of deception in which I had been placed by Sam Wye's malice and my own weakness. What a despicable guy I was really. How could I subject this superb young woman to such duplicity? How could I find it in myself to dupe this excellent creature? How could I take from her that which she treasured most under such basely false pretenses? How, I asked myself, how?

She put down the plate of cake, pressed against me, and kissed me. She was unconfined underneath her house coat. Her lips clung.

My question was answered.

"By God, that's good cake!" I cried hysterically as I pried loose. I started throwing pieces of it down my throat like peanuts. "More!" I bellowed. "More!"

"I'm sorry, dear, there's only enough left for Mother and Dad."

"To hell with them!" I shouted. "Bring me more cake!"

"All right, dear. You're so masterful, so dominating, so frightening. I love it."

She slithered off for more cake. Now she would be coming back with the last of the cake. Now what could I use to stall the inevitable? What a weak wretch I was. What fraudulent gestures I made to salve my flaccid conscience. When you came right down to it, I treated this woman—my true love—exactly the way I would treat a trollop in whom my interest, however acute, was only transient. Was Estherlee, then, a ship that passed in the night? Was she some strumpet, some pickup? "No!" I cried. "No!"

"No what, dear?" called Estherlee from the kitchen.

"Nothing, Estherlee. I was just talking to myself."

"Your poor nerves," she said. "I'll be right out to soothe you."

She was my mate, my life companion, the meaning and purpose of my existence. She would someday be my wife and perpetuate my name. She was the woman I loved and honored. A cad's love! A cad's honor! What an unspeakable lump I was to play fast and loose with such exalted values as virtue, honor, and integrity. How much longer must I act the beast? There must be an immediate end to this cake. There must be a full confession right now.

I rose to my feet. Here and now. This very minute. And not another crumb of cake.

She came in with the cake. "Estherlee," I said, "listen carefully and don't stop me until I'm done."

"All right, dear."

"First I want you to know that I love you."

"I love you too, dear."

"Don't interrupt, please. I love you. My love for you is the motivating force in my life. It explains all my actions—including those which seem incapable of explanation."

"Yes, dear."

"Please. If I am misguided at times, it is only because I let my love for you overshadow my reason. I ask you to judge my conduct in that light. Do you understand?"

"Perfectly, dear. You love me and I love you."

The doorbell rang.

"Of all the damn times," I muttered.

Estherlee answered the door. It was her mother and father. "We got all the way out there," her father said, "and then we remembered that we'd seen the picture."

"It was *Murder the Bastards,*" said her mother. "Have you seen it?"

"Yes," Estherlee answered. "It was wonderful."

They came into the living room. "Hello, Dan," said her father. "It's good to see you. We haven't had a chance to congratulate you." He shook my hand.

"We're terribly proud of you," said her mother.

"It was nothing," I said.

"What's that? Cake?" asked her father. "May I have some, Estherlee?"

"Well, Dad, I don't——"

"Please do," I said hastily.

"Take it upstairs, dear," said her mother. "Good night, children. Aren't you cold in that flimsy house coat, Estherlee?"

"No, Mother. Good night."

"Good night," said her mother.

"Well," said Estherlee when they had gone, "wouldn't you know someone would interrupt while you were proposing?"

"*Proposing!*"

"And it's a good thing you did, too. I was afraid you'd never get around to it. I would have been horribly embarrassed if you hadn't. You see, Mayor La Hoont is announcing our engagement at the bridge blowing tomorrow. He's giving us an engagement ring on behalf of the city. It's supposed to be a secret, but I guess I can tell you now."

I sat down slowly.

"My darling," said Estherlee, drawing me to her breast. "My fiancé. My husband."

She kissed me for a spell, then leaped to her feet and ran to the staircase. "Mother, Dad!" she called. "Come downstairs. We're engaged!"

In all fairness it must be said that I tried.

CHAPTER XX

"Do officers blow up bridges like my son?" demanded Mama, thus ending the argument that had arisen the next morning when I tried to explain to her why I couldn't wear the officer's uniform that she had bought me to wear at the bridge-blowing ceremony. The argument was academic, anyway, because she had taken my G.I. uniform out of the closet while I slept and given it to an old-clothes man.

"There's some silver eagles in the pocket. The man said you wear them on your shoulders. They look nice," she said, and left my bedroom so that I could dress.

What the hell, I told myself as I put on the flesh-pink trousers and the bottle-green coat, I might as well look nice when I end it all. Not that I was panicky about my impending demise; I was beyond panic. The panic had come and gone during the night. Now I was calm in a clammy sort of way. There's no use being scared, I said to myself. The best way to go is the quickest, and what does it all mean anyhow, and life is but a vision between a sleep and a sleep, and (toward the end I began to ramble a little) money doesn't grow on trees, and stuff a cold and starve a fever. Except for occasional pangs that darted into my consciousness like snakes through a fissure, I was calm.

After I dressed (I finally decided not to pin the eagles on my shoulders. No use overdoing it.) I took pen in hand and wrote a will leaving what monies I had to Army Emergency Relief. I left a note for Estherlee bidding her be of good cheer and after a decent interval marry a man of sound eugenic properties. To Sam Wye I wrote a letter assuring him that in my last minutes I bore him no grudge and expressing the hope that he would be able to live a full, happy life even with my blood on his hands. In another letter I implored Mama and Papa to pay closer attention to rationing regulations for the sake of other soldiers, still living. I left instructions for a simple, come-as-you-are interment.

Papa walked in after I had sealed the letters and stacked them on my dresser. "You look nice," he said. "I can't understand why you don't wear that kind of uniform all the time."

"You look nice too," I replied. Indeed he did. He was wearing a new victory suit which included a Sam Browne belt. Binoculars in a leather case hung from the belt.

We went downstairs, where, to Mama's profound delight, I ate a hearty breakfast. Then, while Mama dressed, Papa gave me a fanciful explanation of radio detection, and I assured him that Rand McNally, with whom he contemplated doing some business, were reliable people. Mama came back in her wedding-and-funeral black silk dress, adorned this morning with a huge lavaliere in the shape of a cannon.

"It actually shoots," said Papa.

The shriek of sirens outside announced the arrival of the official party. We went out where a procession of fifteen black limousines escorted by motorcycles was parked at the curb. In the first car sat an animated campaign poster whom I recognized as Mayor La Hoont. As befits a hero, I sat with him. Mama and Papa got in the second car with Estherlee and Mrs. La Hoont. I saw John Smith, Colonel Swatch, and O. Merriam Phyfe in the third car. The rest were filled with civic leaders, aldermen, and suchlike.

"Son," said Mayor La Hoont, giving me a Dale Carnegie

handshake, "it's a fine thing you did." He paused to kiss a passing baby.

"God damn it," said the baby. "I work for Philip Morris."

"A fine thing," repeated His Honor as we screamed out from the curb. "Gad, son, I'd like to be with you boys, but"— he spread out his hands—"the people won't let me go."

The procession traversed the city street by street. Wherever three or more people were gathered the cars stopped while the mayor stood up and led a cheer:

> *"Win, Minn*
> *Win, Minn*
> *Win, Minn*
> *EAPOLIS!"*

Then he threw a handful of cigars in the air and we rolled away.

Halcyon La Hoont could be called a self-made man. His mother, Cosette La Hoont, had not wanted children for two reasons: first, because she was inordinately afraid of pain, and second, because she rightly maintained that her husband Florian's laughable salary as an egg candler was insufficient to raise a child. Nonetheless, on the night of Halley's comet Cosette gave birth to Halcyon. He weighed twenty-two pounds. "Big sonofabitch, ain't he?" remarked Florian, trying to ease the situation with a little jest. Cosette did not answer. Nor did she ever speak another word to Florian. She was that mad.

The infant Halcyon grew up in a sociologist's nightmare. Cosette refused alike to change or nurse him, took up skeet shooting, and began to run with a fast crowd. Florian, doubly despondent because of his wife's behavior and his son's patent hunger, was utterly crushed when the egg candlery installed an electric candler and fired him. Soon after he died of a common cold in three days.

Halcyon lived off his fat for the first year. During his second year, unperceived by his mother, he learned to walk and ran away. He toddled into a saloon, did a self-taught clog, and was rewarded with a pig's knuckle and a glass of bock. Then, as now, no fool, Halcyon stayed. As time went on he added a soft-shoe number and Swedish-dialect stories to his routine. His fame spread. One night a childless alderman named Nate Nye caught his act and bought him.

For the next ten years Halcyon lived with Nate Nye and his infertile wife Norma. He went to school for a time but soon dropped out to spend his days hanging about pool halls and brothels. His foster parents did not discourage him. Nate, who had an alderman's morals, thought it rather cute; Norma, who had never welcomed Halcyon because she believed in her heart that it was Nate, not she, who was barren, didn't give a damn one way or the other.

Halcyon took an early interest in politics. Before he shaved he was a junior ward heeler for Nate Nye. At the age of eighteen he invented a voting machine that automatically defaced opposition ballots. This brought him favorably to the attention of party headquarters. His rise from then on was rapid.

Almost immediately he turned on his benefactor and wrested the alderman's seat from Nate Nye. Brokenhearted, Nate took Norma and retired to Los Angeles, where lo! they were presently blessed with a pair of twins and Nate forthwith became an articulate member of the Chamber of Commerce.

Halcyon progressed. He studied elocution; he learned table manners; he memorized a quarto of Edgar Guest; he married a young socialite whom he caught on the rebound from a shattered romance with a polo enthusiast who had eloped with a woman who owned a secret saddle-soap formula. Inevitably he became the mayor of the city.

Perceiving that Minneapolis was expanding, he acquired through nefarious means the title to a huge swamp outlying the northern city limits. In a gala public ceremony he christened this bog Sunrise Aerie and proclaimed a new housing program. His scheme died a-borning. Prospective builders took one look at Sunrise Aerie and lost interest on the spot. La Hoont was about to write off Sunrise Aerie as a total loss when war came.

Now we were driving up the road to the tremendous ammunition plant that La Hoont had built on Sunrise Aerie. The cars crossed a small wooden bridge (the bridge I was to blow up, I suddenly realized, and the sweat gushed out of my armpits and ran the color in my fuchsia officer's shirt) and pulled up in front of the plant. We got out and took seats on a wooden platform. A crowd jammed the muck in front of the platform, save for one sector where the presence of crocodiles had been reported.

I sat and perspired and stared at the bridge. Its fifteen-foot length looked to me at least as long as the San Francisco Bay bridge; its timbers appeared as solid as the Rock of Ages. A formidable bridge. The grandmother of all bridges. I felt myself turning green.

O. Merriam Phyfe stepped to the front of the platform. "Citizens," he said, "this may well be the greatest day in the history of Minneapolis. For today we are celebrating the completion of the world's largest factory for small-bore ammunition—built in Minneapolis by Minneapolis labor with Minneapolis capital. From this plant in a short time will be rolling more ammunition for more small bores than from any other plant in the world—pending, of course, acceptance of the plant by the War Department, of course, which is, of course, a mere formality, of course.

"I find my words inadequate when I try to tell you of the significance of we Minneapolis folks building this wonderful factory with Minneapolis labor and Minneapolis capital. Therefore I will call now on Minneapolis' poet laureate, John Smith, to read his poem written especially for today's dedication."

Beside the bridge lay a black wooden box, the same kind with which Sam Wye had duped me. Today, however, there would be no hoax. There was dynamite in the box. Death and destruction in a black package. The box lay obscenely in the road and clearly leered at me.

John Smith cleared his throat. *"Bullets, by John Smith,"* he announced. He read:

"A building?
Four walls, a floor, a roof?

Nay.

A challenge, an answer, a promise to young men who blithely risk their lives and live on chow that we who would but cannot join them are in the fray.

" 'Banzai!' cries the Nip.

'Umlaut!' yells the Hun.

From this building, from these four walls, will come the instrument to silence their triumphant expostulations.

"Bullets.

Bullets. Bullets. Bullets.

Bullets. Bullets.

Bullets. Bullets.

Bullets. Bullets. Bullets. Bullets. Bullets.

Bullets.

"Bullets that flew from longbows in colonial times and made of us a nation free.

On San Juan Hill our President's father spoke softly and carried a big bullet.

And what of Sergeant York, huh, what of Sergeant York?

"Here in this place is made revenge.

When an American boy drops into the muzzle of his gun one of the bullets that will soon come from this plant, pending, of course, acceptance by the War Department, he can know that he is ready to fire the wrath of Minneapolis.

"Bullets."

"You certainly expressed the feeling of all of us, Mr. Smith," said O. Merriam Phyfe, resuming the platform. "Now it gives me great pleasure to introduce to you the eminent soldier and military analyst, Colonel Cosmo Fairfax Swatch, who will explain to us the significance of small-bore ammunition in war."

Estherlee, who sat beside me on the platform, tried to hold

my hand, but it slipped out like a wet bar of soap. My eyes were fastened on the bridge and the box of dynamite. I watched them shimmer and inflate until the sky was filled with bridge and box, and from far off I heard a diapason of hellish laughter. I licked my lips, and my tongue running over them made a sound like rustling leaves.

"I would like a lady from the audience," said Colonel Swatch, "to come up on the platform to aid me in a demonstration."

A thin woman started forward.

"Begone, you scrawny wench!" cried the colonel, brandishing his cane. "You over there—the fat one—come up here."

The woman he had indicated waddled up to the platform. The colonel took her arm, then both arms, then he gathered a fold of her back in his hand. "Zum," he murmured. "Satisfactory." He released her and placed a rifle bullet in her hand. "Hold this," he said. "Now, another lady. You in front, come up here."

A globular harridan came to the platform. The old warrior prodded her, took a reading on her behind, pronounced her qualified, and handed her a bullet. Then he called another mountain of flesh, and another and another, until he had exhausted the supply of corpulence. He hummed happily as he worked. When the women were all on the creaking platform he arranged them in ranks. He marched past them in review, stopping before each one to pinch and tweak. One, a retired circus performer, he bit.

With obvious reluctance he finally quit. "Ladies," he said, "you each have in your hand a bullet. That is the product which this plant will produce, pending, of course, acceptance by the War Department. Thank you."

He sat down.

"At this point," said O. Merriam Phyfe in a hushed and solemn voice, "it becomes my almost unbearable pleasure to introduce to you the man who more than any other can be called the soul and essence of Minneapolis, a man who has devoted his years and his energies, without thought of recompense, to the city he loves, to the city that loves him. My dear people,

His Honor, may I say His Excellency, Mayor Halcyon La Hoont."

The mayor held up his hand to silence the applause, although, to be sure, there wasn't any. A few people slapped futilely at the swarms of mosquitoes which rose, even in April, from the bog. "Citizens," said His Honor, "my administration has been notable for many things. Four years ago I installed parking meters that clamped manacles around the ankles of people who put in slugs. Two years ago I erected a pillory in front of City Hall for people who said that Minneapolis was too cold in winter, too hot in summer, too wet in spring and fall. Last year, through my efforts, *Life* magazine sent photographers to cover a Scandinavian wedding in Minneapolis; that the bride's first husband, who had disappeared several years before and was presumed dead but had actually succumbed to a deep-seated urge for a real, old-country smörgåsbord and had gone back to Sweden without remembering to notify his wife, would suddenly reappear during the wedding could not, of course, be foreseen.

"And now this plant, this crowning achievement, this monument to my years of faithful public service. From this plant will soon flow the world's largest output of ammunition, pending, of course, acceptance by the War Department. A mere formality, of course. There has been, I'll admit, some loose talk about the War Department's rejecting this plant because of the ground it is built on. That is plain foolishness.

"There is no better ground in the whole country on which to build a factory of war. For this is hallowed ground. Here were fought battles that made this republic what it is today. Here on this very spot George Custer met and defeated the legions of the treacherous Indian chief, Big Mouth Bigger Nose, who had gone on the warpath because he claimed a passing locomotive had frightened his pregnant squaw and caused her to bear him a son with a tender behind."

"Damn redskins!" shouted Colonel Swatch.

"Here on this very ground was organized the first company

of Minnesota volunteers in the Civil War. One day in late 1865 two hundred young Minnesotans bid their friends and families good-by on this spot and marched South, singing and swinging their carpetbags as they went.

"Now, this is hard to believe, but a naval battle was once fought right here. Yes sir. Impossible as it may seem, there was once a river here. During the War of 1812 the French sloop *Duncan Leprechaun I* sailed up from New Orleans with a cargo of gold bullion with which the French garrison here was to buy the assistance of some Indian tribes."

"Damn redskins!" roared Colonel Swatch.

"A curious fact," continued the mayor. "The *Duncan Leprechaun I* carried eight million dollars' worth of bullion, by a strange coincidence the exact cost of the construction of our present ammunition plant. And damn cheap, too," he added. "Ask anybody who owns an ammunition plant.

"But I digress. A small group of Minnesota scouts learned that the *Duncan Leprechaun I* was approaching, and they knew they must stop it. But how? Aha, my friends, Minnesota ingenuity won the day. They fashioned the first floating mine, a barrel of the whisky that they had brought along to trade with the Indians. The ship hit the barrel, the whisky exploded, and on the very spot where you are standing, my constituents, the *Duncan Leprechaun I* went down with all hands.

"Thus it is obvious that this historic spot is eminently suited for a plant that will be dedicated to the destruction of our enemies.

"And now what could be more fitting than that this dedication ceremony should be highlighted by Minneapolis' own hero, born, bred, and schooled in this city to which I have given all my life, Sergeant Daniel Miller? Sergeant Miller is going to help defeat our enemies here, just as he did in Morocco, by blowing up a bridge. This time it is only a small wooden bridge, not the kind he is accustomed to destroying, but if it is only child's play to the sergeant, to us it is a wonderful thing that our own hero should have a part in our most heroic achievement. Minneapolis is truly grateful that I was able to persuade Sergeant Miller to be with us today.

"And as a token of our gratitude I want to present to Sergeant Miller this diamond ring to give to Miss Estherlee McCracken, to whom he has just become engaged."

Estherlee pushed my slack body upright. The mayor laid the ring in my hand, and it immediately slipped through my trembling fingers. "Isn't that life?" laughed His Honor. "This man isn't a bit afraid of the most dangerous demolition, but he's scared to death of giving his girl a ring. I'll put it on her finger, Sergeant. You go over to the bridge. You'll feel more at ease."

He gave me a little shove that sent me reeling off the platform. Slowly, slowly, with every step a major struggle not to turn and bolt, I walked the hundred feet from the war plant to the bridge. My eyes burned and my throat ached and my stomach churned and the sweat rolled off me in streams. My breath rattled through my open mouth; my elbows and kneecaps twitched. I reached the black wooden box.

I froze like a well-trained pointer. The noise of my heart was roaring in my ears. I bent over and took the top off the box. Inside were four bundles of dynamite sticks, a dozen in a bundle, a box the size of a gasoline can with a handle on top, a bunch of wires, each with a small mechanism at the end, a roll of tape, and another long coil of wire. I trembled anew as I noted each item.

Then I noticed a small card with writing on it on the inside of the box's lid. I lunged at it with a haste that would make a drowning man grasping at straws look hesitant. Perhaps it would tell me what to do with these devil's instruments.

"DANGER—HIGH EXPLOSIVE," it said.

I gnashed my teeth and began to tear the card in half. Suddenly I saw the small print on the back. My salvation! Directions.

"*Take pointed stick and bore hole in top of each dynamite stick. Place cap in hole. Splice cap wires to exploder wire. Unroll to length desired. Attach to exploder. Press plunger.*"

I looked over the box's contents. The dynamite I recognized. The wires with the little things at the end must be the caps. The long coil would be the exploder wire, and the box with the handle the exploder. The tape was for splicing.

All right. Now, how many sticks of dynamite should I use? One on each of the bridge's four supports should do it. Still, one didn't seem like enough. Why would they leave four dozen sticks in the box if all I needed was four? Sure, that's it. I needed four dozen—one dozen for each support. Sure, that was obvious. They even had them bunched up by dozens.

I placed a dozen sticks of dynamite under each of the bridge's four supports.

Now. *Take pointed stick and bore hole in the top of each dynamite stick.* Oh, my God. Boring holes in dynamite sticks. Oh, my God. I took a pencil from my pocket and gingerly pressed the point of it into the top of the dynamite stick. Then I leaped back. All quiet. Well, what the hell. Here goes. I stuck the pencil in deep. Nothing happened. My heart came down from my hard palate. I bored holes in all forty-eight sticks.

Next. *Place cap in hole.* I stuck the tip of each wire into the holes. That's easy. *Splice cap wires to exploder wires.* You know, this is kind of fun. I hummed a little as I gathered the four dozen cap wires and taped them to the long exploder wire.

Unroll to length desired. That's the part I liked best. I picked up the exploder and started walking backward. "Come on, everybody," I called with authority. "Move back with me. Can't have people getting hurt, you know."

Estherlee ran over to my side. "You're wonderful, dear," she said. "So efficient. So calm. I'd be scared to death."

"Oh, pshaw," I murmured.

It was a good long wire. I unrolled and unrolled. The crowd followed me admiringly as I retreated. Mama nudged Papa. "Look, look, our son," she said. I winked at them.

I walked backward with my flock. By God, I said to myself, I'm getting away with it. I'm going to carry it off. I'll blow that little bridge. I *should* with four dozen sticks of dynamite. Jesus, that seems like a lot of dynamite for a little wooden bridge. Well, why did they leave four dozen sticks in the box if I wasn't supposed to use them? It still seems like a lot of dynamite. Well, I've got plenty of wire here. I'll use every inch of it. No use taking chances.

"Move back, folks," I called. "No use taking chances."

I continued walking back. "Nothing like a little walk on a spring morning," I said lightly to Estherlee.

"Darling," she breathed.

The retreat continued. The ammunition plant was getting smaller and smaller. I could scarcely see it now through the mist that hung over the swamp. There was still more wire. I still walked back.

The plant was a speck on the horizon when Colonel Swatch hollered, "God damn it, Sergeant, we're nearing the Dakota line. I've seen men blow bridges ten times that big from a hundred yards. Will you stop?"

"Yeah," called somebody in the crowd. "Where you going?"

"No use taking chances, folks," I said. Another hundred feet of wire remained, and I ran it out. *Attach to exploder*. I did. *Press plunger*. I took the handle in my hands. My confidence suddenly began to ebb. I wiped my forehead. "Give me a kiss, Estherlee," I said.

She gladly complied.

Well, *press plunger*. I pressed.

The air was filled with a noise like a million bowling alleys. The ground trembled, and a pillar of dust and smoke rose from Sunrise Aerie. Then it was still.

Papa took the binoculars from the case on his Sam Browne belt and looked toward the war plant. "Oh, my God, my God!" he cried.

I snatched the glasses from his hands. I looked and didn't believe. I adjusted the glasses, wiped them. No, I was not mistaken.

The ammunition plant was sinking leisurely into the swamp.

Suddenly another object began to emerge beside the war plant. This certainly was a mirage. I watched, transfixed. No. No. It was happening.

As the mire closed over the ammunition factory, up came the *Duncan Leprechaun I!*

CHAPTER XXI

THE PROVOST MARSHAL rang for a guard. "I must admit," he said, "that I've never heard one quite like that. Here, have a cigarette."

I took one and he held a match for me. "You agree, don't you, Captain, that in my case there are certain extenuating circumstances?"

"I agree that there are circumstances. The court-martial will decide how extenuating they are."

"You mean I have to stand trial?"

"Did you expect the Good Conduct Medal?"

"No sir," I said truthfully.

"Naturally you'll have a chance to tell your story to the court. And an officer will be appointed to act as your counsel. His choice will be subject to your approval."

"Yes sir. How do you think I'll come out?"

"Hard to say, Sergeant. It's a rather unusual case."

"Extenuating circumstances?" I asked hopefully.

"Well, circumstances, anyway," he said.

The guard came in and took me off to the guardhouse. We walked through the streets of the camp. All around me I saw soldiers. Everywhere men in uniform. Soldiers, nothing but soldiers.

It was good to be back.